BELLA'S HOME

LEGACY SERIES
BOOK 10

PAULA KAY

CONTENTS

ONE

Isabella turned slightly so that she could see herself in the full-length mirror, gasping a little when she saw her reflection.

"Is that a good sign or a bad one?" Blu said, taking a pin from between her lips to place it where she was cinching the satin material at Isabella's waist.

Before Isabella could reply, she heard Gigi's own gasp from the doorway, followed by Lia's right after.

"Bella, you're so beautiful!" Gigi said.

"We've been counting down the days to see you in this dress." Lia walked over to where Isabella stood on a small stool to take her hand, and Isabella didn't miss the tears in her eyes.

Isabella laughed lightly. "I know. We've kept you all waiting a good long time, haven't we?"

Lia squeezed her hand. "Oh, I don't know. There's nothing wrong with a long engagement."

"Speak for yourself." Gigi winked. "I was beginning to wonder if Douglas and I would—you know—still be around for the wedding day."

"Gi, you're so silly. You and Douglas aren't going anywhere. Well, Douglas isn't anyway—not the way he ran that five miles with me yesterday." Isabella laughed and Gigi leaned in to kiss her on the cheek.

"You have a point there. That man is in the best shape I've seen him in since we were married—despite all the wonderful food Lia's always cooking for us," said Gigi.

"It's the Tuscan air." Lia smiled at Gigi. "And our morning walks are paying off for you too. Don't pretend that you're not feeling—and looking—pretty wonderful yourself, young lady."

Isabella looked back down at Blu and the two smiled at one another—it was the silent shared acknowledgment of how great it always felt to be all together.

"Well? I'm still waiting on your thoughts there, little miss bride-to-be. There's still a lot of work to be done, of course, but what do you think so far?"

"Ooh, it's better than I ever imagined. Thank you again—so much, Blu—for making my dress—for making all the dresses for me. I still can't believe that you really have the time."

Blu winked at her. "I'll always make time for you and—well, to repeat Gigi's point, I've had a few years to play with the sketches."

They all laughed and Isabella pulled her hair back away from her face as she looked into the mirror at herself and the other women sitting nearby. "Well, you know me. We wanted to wait until Thomas was finished with school—until we had a good idea of where we'd end up once we were married."

Isabella didn't miss the look that passed between Lia and Gigi. "Wait. What's that look for, you two?"

"Oh, nothing," said Gigi.

Blu took the final pin out from between her lips and whispered loud enough for everyone in the room to hear. "Every time you leave the villa, these two talk about how much they want you to stay forever."

"Believe me, it's hard for me to leave too," said Isabella.

Over the past few years, since she and Thomas had gotten engaged, they'd spent Christmases and most of the summers at

Lia's and Antonio's. After some fantastic European vacations, Isabella's parents had surprised everyone when they'd decided to sell their house in Connecticut to move to a sweet little village on the coast of Spain. And they too, would often come to Tuscany to stay in one of the many guest houses that Lia and Antonio had added to their property.

When Isabella stopped to think about it, it was a little odd that she and Thomas would be choosing to settle down in Connecticut after all their travels, but she felt that she had to support his decisions when it came to his career.

Thomas had always supported her throughout the years, and Isabella had done her share of waffling back and forth when it came to her settling in New York City. Finally, she'd gotten an apartment and spent time in the city near Thomas about as much as she did away traveling. And they'd made it work, Thomas getting through his studies and Isabella marking off the spots on Arianna's map.

She grinned thinking about the map. She'd brought it with her to Italy. Gigi, especially, always seemed to enjoy looking at it with her—hearing about her adventures as Isabella shared pictures and stories about her travels.

"Sorry, what did you say, Gigi?"

Gigi laughed, probably at the funny expression on Isabella's face as she'd zoned out thinking about everything under the sun.

"I was just reminding you that I want to see the pictures of the house."

Isabella nodded. "Oh, yes. I have them on my phone."

"How many bedrooms did you say it has?"

"Four bedrooms and an apartment above the garage." This time Isabella definitely saw a look pass between Gigi and Lia. She laughed. "Yes, I know. Plenty of room for an expanding family."

"Well, it can't hurt to be ready." Lia grinned at Isabella.

Isabella's thoughts turned back to Thomas and their new home. He'd gone to so much trouble to find just the right house for them—a house that Isabella would love. And she had loved it when she'd seen it—she'd agreed that living there, a doable commute from what would be Thomas's new office, made sense for them.

Thomas would be working in management for his father's company and Isabella could write from anywhere—Thomas had said that they'd set up the space above the garage to be her office. And they'd keep Isabella's apartment in the city—for Thomas's business meetings there and also as a place they could go to when they wanted a little getaway from the slower pace of the suburbs.

Without meaning to, Isabella sighed loud enough that all the women in the room turned to look at her.

"You okay? You're probably about ready to get out of that, huh?" Blu asked her.

Isabella turned to look out the nearby window. "Well, I think the guys will be in soon. Thomas and I have a date to go over the final items we need to do here before we leave for New York."

"Where'd they go so early this morning?" asked Gigi.

"I think Antonio wanted to go look at that property just up for sale." Lia winked at Gigi. "You know, the one I was saying that you and Douglas should think about."

Gigi laughed. "You mean, the vineyard next door to you? I don't want to speak for that energetic husband of mine, but I'm pretty confident that learning the fine art of wine-making is not a challenge we're up for at this stage in our lives."

Isabella grinned at them. "Lia, I don't think you'll be happy until we are all moved in right here with you at the vineyard."

Lia laughed too. "Well, I'd say you got that right. But okay, I'll settle for having Gigi in town. Now, my Bella so far away in Connecticut—that's another story, my dear."

Isabella felt a little wave of sadness. It was how she always felt when she it was time to leave Tuscany. "I know. But I'll be back before you know it. There's still too much to do to stay away for long."

Lia crossed the room to give Isabella a light kiss on the cheek. "You pay no attention to me, my dear. I know your priorities are right. Thomas is lucky to have you there supporting him and his career. We'll just have to take your visits when we can get them."

Blu had stepped back with a critical look on her face as she examined Isabella in the dress. "Well, it sure sounds like the newlyweds will have room for us in the new house. Not to invite ourselves, but I wouldn't say no to a visit." She winked at Isabella.

"Oh, you know I will love to have you all come visit. I'm going to hold you to that." Isabella turned to Lia as she took Blu's hand to step down from where Blu had been working on her dress. "And Lia, you will always be a priority for me—for both of us. We love coming here, and that's not going to stop after we're married."

Lia reached out to squeeze Isabella's hand. "I know, honey. Your grandfather and I are delighted with how often you visit. You just focus on that lovely husband-to-be. Speaking of which, Antonio just texted me that they are on their way home, so let's get you out of that dress."

Isabella followed Blu behind the partition she'd set up, hugging her tight before she stepped out of the dress. "The dress is really gorgeous. I can't express to you how much I love it. I feel just like a princess."

"As you should, lovely girl." Blu looked her in the eyes. "I can't wait to see the look on your young man's face when he sees you. You're going to be a beautiful bride, Bella."

Isabella smiled as Blu left her to change back into her clothes. She still had to pinch herself about the fact that she was marrying Thomas—the man of her dreams and the best friend she'd ever had.

TWO

Gigi set the coffee down in front of her friend at the small breakfast table that overlooked the vineyard outside. Since moving to Tuscany two years ago, she and Lia had gotten into the wonderful routine of having coffee together at least a few mornings every week. The two women had only grown closer over the years, and Gigi could hardly imagine a time when they'd not known one another.

She reached across the table to place her hand on Lia's as her friend looked out the window, seemingly lost in her own thoughts. "Lia, are you okay? I can hold down the fort here if you want to go have a rest."

Lia smiled back at her. "Thank you. We'll just take a break here with our coffee for a few minutes and I'll be just fine. So, how stunning did our Bella look in that dress?"

Gigi felt her eyes instantly go wet with tears. Seeing Isabella in her wedding gown had literally taken her breath away. "I still don't know how Blu manages to do that, but it's the most gorgeous dress I've ever seen. And—well, Bella would look beautiful, no matter the dress, but indeed she looks like something out of the pages of a young girl's fairy tale."

"That's exactly what I was thinking." Lia nodded her head toward where the men stood talking outside in the vineyard not far from the house. "That young man is in for a wonderful treat."

Gigi nodded, also watching Thomas from the window as he grinned at the two men who'd seemed to become pretty important in his life since his engagement to Isabella.

"Douglas thinks the world of Thomas. The way that he jumped right in to help him with the rebuilding last summer said an awful lot about his character."

While Isabella and Thomas had been spending the previous summer at the vineyard, a terrible storm had done a lot of destruction to several of the main buildings at the orphanage. When Douglas had made plans to immediately fly to Guatemala, Thomas had been right beside him, no questions asked.

Lia was nodding in agreement. "Yes, Antonio also feels nothing but happy for Thomas to be joining our family officially." Lia looked across the table at Gigi, and Gigi didn't miss the gleam in her eye as she spoke her next words. "Antonio says that Thomas has a real knack for the business. He's very quick to pick things up and his interest has only seemed to grow stronger over the past year."

"I hope he'll be happy working for his father," said Gigi. "That it's what he really wants to do, I mean."

"Yes, that's exactly what Antonio and I have talked about. It's not our place to pry, and Bella doesn't share too much about it. She seems happy, though—with their plans—do you think so, Gigi?"

Gigi was thoughtful. They'd all been pretty careful when it came to Isabella's and Thomas's relationship. Isabella had shared with them some angst that she'd felt over the past years whenever she'd been living in New York City. It didn't feel like home to her, and the struggle had always been about how much time to spend there with Thomas versus traveling or spending time abroad with her family. In the end, of course, it was their decision to make, and

Isabella's family understood her feelings of wanting to support Thomas with his career goals.

Gigi looked back over at Lia, who was waiting for a response from her. "Yes, I think she's happy with their plans." Gigi trusted that, more than anything, Thomas wanted Isabella to be happy. They'd work it out and the family would continue to enjoy long holidays and vacations together when they could.

Blu walked across the room, carrying her own cup of coffee to the table. "Ah, great minds think alike." She bent down to give Lia a quick hug and then leaned in to kiss Gigi on the cheek before joining the women at the table. She grinned over at them both. "Is it just me, or was Bella absolutely breathtaking in that dress? I mean, not to toot my own horn or anything." She smiled as she glanced down at the pictures she'd taken on her phone. "I have to say it..." She held her phone out, first for Gigi to see and then Lia. "Does she not look just like Ari?"

Lia smiled back at Blu. "I was thinking exactly the same thing about my beautiful granddaughter."

"The fact that we get to celebrate such a wonderful occasion with her feels a little bit like a miracle, doesn't it?" Gigi said.

So many years had passed since Arianna's death. Mostly now when they talked about her, Gigi was able to do so with fond memories and less sadness. Having Isabella in their lives years later had helped to heal so much of the remnants of the grief they'd all carried.

Lia smiled and looked out the window toward Antonio. "Yes, she's most definitely a miracle to us. One that I will be forever grateful for."

Blu, never one to hide her emotions, was watching Lia. Gigi could read the concern in her eyes as Blu reached her hand out to touch Lia gently on the arm.

"Lia, how are you doing? You'd tell us, wouldn't you? If it's too much having us all here?"

Lia was just as quick to show Blu a big smile. "Nonsense. I'm fine and everything is good. Having you all here is exactly what I need right now, so don't even for a second think that it's not the case."

"Okay, but we're here to help. Don't forget that. And Chase is arriving tomorrow with big plans for a dinner feast. I think you're really going to like the latest additions to his menu at the restaurant. He's been dying to make them for you."

Lia smiled. "I can't wait." She glanced toward the clock on the wall behind her. "Let's see...Emily and Richard are due here any minute. And Chase will be here with the girls by late afternoon. Is that right?"

"Yes, he told me today that Gabby and Kylie have had the best week at camp—so much so that they've been begging to go for another session," Blu said.

Lia laughed. "Yes, Gabriela mentioned that to me on the phone as well. I told her we'd talk about it after we've had her home for at least the weekend."

"Right. I was thinking, though, that it might make good sense for our trip down south. We could go for the first three weeks or so and then Chase or Antonio could bring the girls down for the rest of the time."

"So does this mean that you got the house you were telling us about? The one with the incredible view?" Gigi said.

"The one with the incredible kitchen?" Lia winked.

"I did indeed," said Blu. "It's going to be spectacular, with plenty of room for all of us and more to spare. It will be the perfect place for me to work on finishing the dresses, and I've already talked to Jemma. She's coming a few days after we arrive and I think she really wants it to be a surprise for Isabella."

"Well, I guess that's the question of the day, really." Gigi took a sip of her coffee. "Have you said anything to Bella yet?"

"Aha. I knew my ears were burning for a reason." Isabella laughed as she walked across the room to take the last available seat at the table. She turned toward Gigi. "Has who said what to me?"

Blu grinned and leaned over to give Isabella a quick hug. "Well, I—we, really—wanted to surprise you with a little getaway. I know that you've not really spent that much time at the Amalfi Coast, and I've rented the most beautiful big villa for us all in Positano for several weeks. We figured that it could be an extended wedding shower of sorts for you. We'll eat lovely food and drink lovely wine and I'll finish the dresses—"

"—Which will also be quite lovely." Lia laughed as she interrupted her friend.

"And Bella, I know you're planning to head back after the weekend, but we're hoping that you can change your plans—maybe just stay here with us until the wedding," Blu grinned.

Gigi was watching Isabella carefully. She saw the way the young girl's face lit up when Blu mentioned the Amalfi Coast, but she also knew that Isabella and Thomas had some major things to take care of back home, not the least of which was the closing on their new home in Connecticut. And she knew the look of Isabella's trying to hold back tears. That was the look that she saw now.

"You all are so sweet to do this. Any other time, I'd jump at the chance, but I just don't see how I could make that happen. We've got to get back to pack up the remaining things from my apartment and close on the house. Maybe I can come out a few weeks earlier if you're still there? But I shouldn't say yes until I speak to Thomas about it. I know that he had some other things that he wanted us to get done before we come back out for the wedding, and—well, I have been traveling already a lot this year." She laughed lightly. "I don't want him to feel that I'm choosing travel —or Italy—over him every time."

Blu leaned over to give Isabella a hug. "Don't worry, Bella. We knew that it might not work with your plans, and I understand. Talk to Thomas and just let us know if anything will work for you. Gigi, Lia, and I will be there for the month, and it's looking like the kids will come join us for the last week or so—after their camp lets out."

Gigi reached across the table to squeeze Isabella's hand. "Talk to Thomas, and only if it feels like the right thing to do, okay, honey?"

Isabella nodded her head and stood up to walk over to the window, her face lighting up in a big smile. "My parents are here!"

THREE

Isabella hadn't seen her parents for a few months and was taken aback by the emotion she felt as she hugged them close. Their new Spanish lifestyle definitely seemed to be agreeing with them. She linked her arm through her mom's as they followed her father to the outside patio, where Lia had scooted them out so that they could have some privacy.

"You both look so happy and healthy! I guess you've found the time you were wanting, to hang out at that lovely beach of yours."

Emily nodded her head and took Richard's hand across the table as they sat down. "Oh, honey, we love the new house so much. Please tell me that you and Thomas are going to be coming for a visit soon."

Isabella grinned. "Well, maybe you need to talk to Thomas about that. He's in charge of the honeymoon, but he did give me the hint that it will be in Europe, so swinging down your way is a distinct possibility, I suppose."

"How much time will you have? For the honeymoon?" Richard asked.

"Thomas won't start work until mid-October, so I think he's

figuring that we'll take the whole month after our wedding." Isabella laughed lightly.

"What is it, honey?" Emily asked.

"I just shocked myself hearing those words come out of my mouth." Isabella grinned. "I mean, would you ever have thought that Thomas and I..." She took in the look that passed between her parents.

"Well, actually, yes." Richard laughed and squeezed his wife's hand. "I can remember one day—I think you were probably around thirteen or so—the two of you had come running into the house after ice skating or sledding—something that had your cheeks all rosy and away from your studies for a few hours."

Isabella sat forward in her chair a bit, enjoying herself as the faint recollection came to her mind.

"Your father and I were watching the two of you all cozy with your hot chocolate as you sat together on the sofa laughing and teasing one another about one thing or another," Emily said.

"We couldn't hear your conversation, but Thomas reached out to put a bit of hair behind your ear—"

"—And it was such a tender moment." Emily interrupted, her eyes suddenly wet with tears.

"Your mother looked at me and pulled me back into the kitchen to whisper that somewhere along the way, our Izzy had become loved by that young man."

Isabella smiled as countless bits of memories from her childhood with Thomas flashed through her mind. She'd always felt loved by Thomas. She looked at her father. "And you weren't at all sure that Thomas would be a good choice for me."

"Well, not then maybe, I'll admit. But Thomas is a fine young man." Richard looked across the table to catch Emily's eye. "And your mother and I couldn't be more happy to have him as a part of our family."

"He's your soulmate, that's for sure. I never doubted it after that day," Emily said.

"Well, it sure seems like the two of you were clued in before we ever were." Isabella laughed. "Thank goodness fate had its way and paid no attention to everything he and I did to nearly mess things up between us."

"You're together now, and that's what matters." Emily smiled. "And honey, Blu sent me pictures from earlier—of you in your dress. You look absolutely divine in it."

"Do you think so? I'm sorry we couldn't wait for you. I'll try it on again before you leave, though. I really want you to see it."

Emily laughed. "Absolutely. I refuse to leave without seeing you in it for myself."

"I'm so glad you were able to come. It's going to be hard to leave in a few days—what with so much yet to get done. But Lia and Gigi—and Blu—have been so incredibly helpful. They assure me that they've got everything under control, and I guess Thomas and I need to spend the next few weeks focusing on everything back home."

Isabella tried not to show her emotions as she spoke. She'd made a promise to herself to be excited about the new house and everything that was to come along with their marriage in just a few short months. She owed that to Thomas—to be fully supportive of him as he started out in his new job.

"Honey, what's that look for?" Richard asked as he reached out to touch Isabella's arm. "Is everything okay?"

"Oh, yeah. Everything's fine. Really."

"But?"

"We know that look, Iz," Emily said. "Is it the move?"

When she and Thomas had made the decision—after much debate—that he was going to work for his father for at least a year after graduating NYU, Isabella had had long phone conversations with her mother. Emily had asked her all the hard questions which had helped Isabella to get to a place of recognizing that it was a time for her to be willing to compromise—that there would be plenty of time for Thomas and her to travel—and because she could write from anywhere, it only seemed right that their location be dependent on what Thomas felt was the best move for his career.

Isabella knew all this with her head, but her heart seemed to be tripping her up a bit when it came to being excited about the new house and the move to Connecticut.

She looked back over at her parents, who were waiting for her response. "Yes, I suppose it is the move. I am very happy to be getting out of the city—that's for sure. And I know I'll be happy wherever I am—as long as I'm with Thomas. I mean, it's not like he won't be supportive of me visiting my family or taking the occasional trip that I might need for writing research, but..."

"But what, honey?" Richard asked. "You're not having second thoughts about getting married, are you?"

"Oh, no. You don't have to worry about that, Dad. That's the one thing I don't have doubts about." She smiled and then laughed at the look of relief on her father's face. "What? Were you actually thinking I was going to become some runaway bride or something?"

Richard laughed too. "No, not really. It's just that we know how stressful wedding preparations can be. It can take a toll on even the strongest of couples. Bottom line is that your mother and I are here to support you, whatever that might mean."

"And we'd be completely devastated if you were to call off the wedding to our soon-to-be wonderful son-in-law," Emily said.

"Well, good. I guess we're all on the same page with that then." Isabella winked.

"Okay then, before I interrupted you earlier, you did seem about to tell us what it is that's on your mind."

Isabella nodded. She wanted to be careful when it came to talking about Thomas. She respected the boundaries of their relationship and she never wanted to talk to others about things that they should be discussing between themselves. But she so desperately wanted Thomas to get the same satisfaction from his career that she had managed to find with her writing. And deep inside, she felt that his working for his father was going to be a mistake—that it wasn't really something that he was passionate about.

"Well, I just want Thomas to be happy with what he's doing." Isabella looked past her parents to the vineyard where she could see Thomas walking with Antonio, his shoulders broad and his arms tanned from being outside every day for the past weeks of the summer.

Emily's eyes followed Isabella's. "Well, to see him here, it is hard to imagine him in some office wearing a suit and tie."

"So, I'm not crazy, right? I can't tell you how many times we've talked about how much he loves being here at the vineyard—with Antonio—with everyone, but especially he and Antonio spend so much time together, talking about the business. After every time we come, I'm amazed at how much he's learned. He really does seem to love it."

"So is it something you've talked to Antonio about? Would it be an option for you two to live here?" Richard laughed when he saw the look on Emily's face. "Okay, let me rephrase that, because I know that your grandparents would be over-the-moon to have you here permanently. I guess Thomas must feel that he needs to be working with his dad before he does anything else, and I can understand that."

Isabella nodded. "Yes, I think so, but the funny thing is, I know that his father would completely understand if Thomas didn't want to go into the business with him. I think it's just something that's been understood between them for so long. I'm not sure. Of course we've talked about it and I do feel that Thomas can be a bit stubborn—but so can I—I'm aware." Isabella sighed. "It's just weird because both of us know that I have enough money from Arianna's trust to support us with whatever we want to do. I guess it's just a guy thing maybe?"

Richard winked at her and reached out once more for Isabella's hand this time. "Honey, I think that absolutely could be a guy thing, as you say—but one that could be very important to him. You have always said how much it's meant to you that he's always been there for you, taking care of you, throughout practically all your childhood years."

Emily was nodding. "I think maybe he still wants to be that knight in shining armor—the provider for his bride."

Isabella grinned. "Well, he is my knight in shining armor. That's not going to change. I think maybe we just need to talk more about it. The only thing that matters to me is that he's doing something that is going to make him feel happy and satisfied—whatever that is."

"That's right, honey. You're going to make a fine wife. Your mother and I couldn't be prouder of you." Richard stood up and extended his hand to Emily. "Now, speaking of happy and satisfied, Lia whispered to me that she was preparing a lunch for us around two. Shall we go have a little rest before then?"

Emily nodded, and Isabella laughed as she too stood up from the table. "It's nice to see this new relaxed retirement phase that you two seem to be enjoying—naps and all." She hugged her parents. "Thanks again so much for coming. You go rest and I'll see you at lunch in a few hours."

FOUR

Blu looked up toward the sound of the light knock on the open door to see Isabella standing in the doorway.

Isabella grinned. "Can I come in?"

"Yes, of course. In fact I want to show you what I'm working on." Blu released the garment she'd been sewing, then stood up and held it out for Isabella to see.

"Oh wow. Jemma is going to look so gorgeous in that, but..."

"But what?" Blu laughed and turned the front of the dress around so that she could see it.

"Well, I think it might be just a tad big for Jem, don't you think?"

"Oh—well, I'm going by the measurements she sent me." Blu saw the look of confusion on Isabella's face and laughed as she tried to think of how to respond. "She did say that she'd put on a bit of weight since their wedding."

"Oh, right. She mentioned that to me too." Isabella crossed the room to run her fingers over the blue satin fabric. "I love the color so much. It's going to look stunning outside, isn't it?"

Blu looked toward the big window, where she had a perfect view of the vineyard outside. When Lia had first showed her the room that she'd had designed specifically for Blu's workspace when she visited, Blu had felt a rush of emotion and a flash to another moment in time.

It had been one of those moments that happened every so often between her and Lia. History repeating itself and worthy of the instant tears so many years later.

When Arianna had first taken Blu to the beach house in San Diego, she'd had a similar room with a view that couldn't have been more dissimilar to the one she had here, but equally as breathtaking.

"Yes, I love the color you chose. And it's all going to be stunning—this spectacular wedding of yours, my dear." Blu gently placed the gown on a table along one wall of the room and then turned to take Isabella's hand. "Come sit with me for a minute."

The two settled in on the small sofa in the corner of the room, where they had the same expansive view of the vineyard outside.

"I love this room so much. Well, all the rooms have fantastic views, don't they?" Isabella said.

"They do. Yes. And Lia is always so thoughtful as a hostess. I still don't know how she manages to get the most perfect flower arrangements in all the rooms—even when I end up coming with little notice."

Isabella reached out to gently touch the colored assortment of flowers that sat in the middle of the coffee table in front of them. "Oh, I can tell you the answer to that question." She laughed. "It's that special relationship she has the with the flower shop owner down the street from the restaurant. Complimentary lunches at Thyme in exchange for emergency flower arrangements."

Blu smiled as she watched Isabella lean back into the sofa, pulling her legs underneath her as she did so. She still marveled at it sometimes—the fact that she—and everyone—had this wonderful relationship with Arianna's daughter. It was something that would have made her best friend so pleased to know if they'd had a crystal ball back when Ari had become sick.

"So tell me, Bella, how are you feeling about everything? All your plans seem to be moving along nicely. I know that Chase intends to sit down with you tomorrow to go over the menu. I think he's done a very good job choosing your favorites."

Isabella smiled back at her. "Yes, I'm actually not feeling very stressed about the wedding—thanks to you all, of course. You all are the best wedding planners a girl could ask for. I know that the dresses, the flowers, the food—it's all going to be perfect..."

Blu waited a few seconds before she spoke, eyeing Isabella and trying to read her body language. Isabella wasn't good at hiding her emotions, something that Blu and the others had come to appreciate about her over the years. And Blu was always happy to be a sounding board for Isabella, just as she was for Jemma. The two young girls meant everything to Blu and the other women in their lives, and they'd all move mountains to ensure their happiness.

"But?" Blu touched Isabella gently on the arm. "I definitely feel that there's a but there. What's going on?"

"Oh, I don't know. I just had a conversation with my parents —about Thomas—and I suppose it's got my mind going a bit."

"Is it something you want to talk through?"

Isabella seemed thoughtful as she looked at Blu across from her. At opposite ends of the sofa, with their feet tucked up and their toes touching, they could have been girlfriends about to have a gossip session. But Blu knew that Isabella valued her advice, and with Jemma gone, she welcomed these times, wanting to be a surrogate mother of sorts for Isabella whenever she needed someone to listen to her.

"Yeah, I don't know exactly what's bothering me or how to put it into words, really." Isabella seemed to be studying Blu for a moment. "Can you tell me about Chase? What it was like when you first got together?"

"About our relationship, you mean?"

"Well, yeah, but what I really want to know is how you two

made decisions about work. I'm guessing that neither of you have to work really—because of what Arianna gave us, I mean."

"Ah, the same way that you and Thomas are going to have a bazillion choices about what you want your life together to look like, you mean." Blu smiled as Isabella nodded her head.

"I suppose that's one way to put it, yes."

"Well, the thing with me was that my designs and fashion had always been so important to me. And Ari had always been such a big supporter of it all. In the beginning, I worked very hard to get my line going. Over time, as you know, I've cut back a lot. Time with Kylie seems to go by so quickly and I don't want to miss things with her." She grinned. "But I love it. I always will, so it never feels like work to me."

"And what about Chase? Did he ever think of not working once you two were married?"

"Oh, no. Chase loves being in the kitchen in the same way I love being in my designing space. It's part of who he is, and I don't think he could ever stop cooking for people. It makes him too happy—it's what seems to satisfy him the most, I guess you could say. Well, the kids and I probably make it to a good second on his list, but cooking is definitely his passion." Blu laughed.

"Yeah, that's the key word—or emotion—isn't it? Passion. It's what I do feel when I'm writing—what I've always felt with my writing."

"But you're wondering about that fiancé of yours, I take it?"

Isabella nodded. "I just want him to feel good about what he's doing, you know?"

"Do you think that he doesn't want to work for his dad?"

"No, I don't think it's so much that he doesn't want to. It's more that I see him so much happier when we're traveling or when we're staying here with Lia and Antonio. Back home, he always seems a bit stressed to me. In fairness, though, I'm sure it will change now that he's done with school—once we start our 'real life' together." Isabella laughed as she used air quotes with her words.

"I think it's nice that you're concerned about him in that way."

Isabella looked down, and Blu didn't miss the look that passed quickly on her face.

"Well, I have to be honest with myself, though—not to make it about me and my less-than-excited feelings about living in Connecticut. I guess you could say that I may have caught the travel bug over these last few years." Isabella laughed.

"Well, there are worse things than having a passion for travel." Blu grinned. "Would it help you to feel better if you guys stayed in New York?"

"Oh no, I'm way done with living in the city. The house in Connecticut was the biggest selling point for me with his job. We are keeping my apartment, though, just because it's nice to have for when we do want to be in town for any length of time. I'm going to enjoy the extra space in the house and it really is quite lovely." Isabella sighed.

Blu reached out to grab Isabella's hand. "The two of you will figure it out. And you know what I've come to know over the years, Bella, my dear?"

"What's that?"

"Nothing is ever carved in stone. We're allowed to change our minds, to make different decisions as we change and grow—as individuals and as couples. And the cool thing for you is that Arianna wanted that for you—the freedom to be able to choose the things you want in life that will make you happy."

Isabella leaned in to give Blu a hug. "You're right. I need to just let go of it all—to enjoy these next few months. It's my old worrying self rearing its ugly head again." Isabella laughed as she stood up.

"Well, you wouldn't be the first bride to worry a bit about what the future is going to look like. I agree, though, let yourself bask in all the good things that are coming to you. We all can't wait to celebrate your marriage and officially welcome that young man into our family. We're all very happy for you, Bella."

Isabella gave Blu one last squeeze before she left the room, and Blu smiled as she watched her go.

Yes, Isabella and Thomas would figure it all out, and if the rest of them were very lucky, they'd be seeing even more of Isabella as time progressed. If Blu were a betting woman, she'd put money on that fact.

FIVE

Isabella grabbed her phone and her jacket as she headed out the door. She texted Thomas—who'd gone somewhere with Antonio —that she'd be back in an hour. They still needed to chat about a few final decisions that needed to be made before they left Tuscany in a few days.

She put her jacket on and did a few stretches before she headed down the long driveway of the vineyard. The temperature was just the way she liked it—nice and fresh—with the sun bright in a cloudless sky. Isabella hadn't been as strict with her running schedule as she'd been in the past, but whenever she was in Tuscany, she liked to take advantage of the gorgeous countryside.

She couldn't help but compare it to her running routine in New York City, which was the complete opposite. Even when she did manage to make it across town to Central Park, it was way busier there than the busiest times where she ran in Italy.

There was no denying the fact that she was not a city girl, at least not in terms of long-term living. In that respect, Connecticut would be better for her. She could live with that.

Her thoughts went to her mental checklist for everything that needed to be done back home. Thomas had already sold his place.

His apartment was much bigger than Isabella's, but they'd agreed that it made more sense for their needs and the location to hold on to Isabella's place in the city.

Their closing date on the Connecticut house was coming up in less than two weeks and the movers were scheduled for just a few days later. It was a lot to get done while also planning the wedding from afar, but after numerous discussions, and assurances from Lia, Gigi, and Blu, Isabella felt confident that everything would be moving ahead smoothly by the time she arrived a few weeks before the wedding.

She smiled as she thought about her dress. The fitting that morning had been the first time that she'd had it on while it had all been in one piece. She'd had so much fun looking over Blu's sketches over the past year or so, and though the women teased her about how long her engagement had been, there was an easiness to it all that had been fun for Isabella. And in the end, she knew that the gown Blu was designing for her was going to be more magical than she ever could imagine.

Annie, as the flower girl, had an absolutely adorable dress, also made by Blu. Of all the unexpected surprises that had come with meeting her birth father, Lucas, meeting her sister had been one of the most special. And they'd all only grown closer over the past years.

The only other person she was having in the actual wedding was Jemma as her Matron of Honor—something that Jemma had accepted gleefully. She'd promised that she would arrive a full two weeks before the wedding so that she could throw Isabella some kind of fantastic little bachelorette party—Tuscan style.

Isabella stopped running to pull her ringing phone out of her pocket. She hit the accept button of her video chat app and waited for her friend's face to appear on her screen.

"Jemma! How did you know I was just thinking about you?"

Jemma laughed and her smiling face filled up the screen. "Were you? I hope you're not too mad at me for not being there with you all right now."

"Are you kidding? I wouldn't dream of taking you guys away from the orphanage. The kids need you and as long as I get you for the big day, I can handle that."

Jemma and Rafael had taken over at the orphanage for the past two months while Tori had had to go to the U.S. to care for her sick mother. Isabella had thought it pretty incredible for Rafael to insist that he could manage when Douglas had been preparing to go himself.

"Well, you can count on me. Oh, I can't wait to see you. I really miss you all so much."

"I miss you too. It always feels so weird for me to be here without you."

"Are you outside? It's so sunny!"

"Yeah, just taking a little run while I wait for Thomas to come back."

"Shirking his wedding planning duties?" Jemma winked.

"Oh, you know. He gets with Antonio and those two could talk wine and business all day long. I heard Antonio speaking earlier about a meeting with a buyer, so I suppose he let Thomas tag along."

"That's great—that they all get along so well with him, right?"

"I guess we've both done pretty well in that department, huh? In terms of choosing our husbands wisely?" Isabella laughed as Rafael came into the picture to sneak a quick kiss from Jemma.

"Hey, Bella. How are you doing? Everything coming together for the big day?"

"Hi, Raf. It is, yes. I was just telling Jem that it doesn't seem the same without you both here. I hope you two will be able to get away to come early before the wedding."

"Yes, we'll be there." Jemma looked quickly at Rafael. "Well, we're waiting to hear back from Tori, but she's due back within the next few weeks."

Rafael waved toward the camera. "On that note, I gotta get back to the kids. We miss you, and please give Thomas and everyone our best."

Isabella watched as he gave Jemma a quick kiss before leaving. Jemma looked tired, but who wouldn't be, overseeing an entire orphanage?

When Isabella and Thomas had visited the orphanage for the first time a few years ago, Isabella had been awed by how everything ran and how sweet the children were. She instantly knew what the draw had been for Gigi and Douglas, and it made her appreciate them that much more.

"How are *you* doing, Jem? Don't take offense at this, but you look pretty wiped out."

"Do I?" Jemma reached up to smooth her hair back from her face. "Well, it is all pretty exhausting, to be honest, but it makes Rafael very happy to be able to help here and of course, it makes me happy too. It will just feel good when I can get a regular night's sleep again—and some more structured painting time—but enough about how I am. I'm happy to hear that you're having fun there, and it sounds like the planning isn't too stressful. And the house? All of that is on track?"

"Oh yeah. All systems go. We should be able to move in by the end of the month, I'd say."

"You say that with such enthusiasm—and I'm not sure if you're aware or not, but you also wrinkled your nose."

Isabella laughed. "Did I?"

Jemma nodded. "You did."

"Well, it's nothing we've not already talked about. I am feeling better about things, in fact. I guess I need to do a better job of showing that, huh?"

"Yeah, you might need to work on that poker face of yours."

Isabella laughed. She told Jemma pretty much everything, and they'd had long talks about how Isabella felt in regards to her future plans for settling down in Connecticut.

"I really am okay about it. As long as Thomas is doing what he thinks makes the most sense for his career, I need to support that. And that is something I learned by your example, you know."

Years ago, before Jemma and Rafael had become a couple, Jemma had loaned Rafael money so that he could open his dream business. It was only after they'd been married a year—just a few months ago—that Rafael finally agreed that the business loan was null and void—it was their business and Jemma's inheritance was what she brought to their marriage for both of them. This was the way Jemma had wanted it from the beginning, but she had to learn to bite her tongue when it came to understanding that Rafael wanted to financially support their life together as well.

Isabella had admired the way that Jemma had gone to Guatemala to live and work alongside Rafael, not because they needed the money, but because it was what he'd always wanted. So she'd taken all that to heart, thinking about her own relationship with Thomas and what his own goals were.

"Well, Thomas is lucky to have you—you're lucky to have one another, I should say."

"Speaking of which..." Isabella waved to Antonio's truck slowing down as he grew nearer. "Here comes Thomas now. I think I better grab a ride back to the house with them. He and I need to finalize a few things before we leave here."

"Okay. Bella?"

"Yes?" Isabella grinned into the phone just as Antonio and Thomas pulled over to the side of the road across from her.

"You're going to be the most beautiful bride. I can't wait to see you soon. And I really miss you."

"I miss you too, Jem. Big hugs! And see you soon!"

Isabella clicked off the video chat and crossed the road to lean into the passenger side window where Thomas sat grinning at her.

"You need a ride, li'l lady?"

"Why, yes. If you kind sirs are offering."

"We only pick up the prettiest girls."

Isabella giggled as Thomas opened the door and pulled her in onto his lap.

"Yes, I think you just might be the prettiest one we've picked up all morning."

"Very funny!" She playfully punched him on the arm and they made their way back to the villa.

SIX

Lia stood by the big breakfast window, sipping her tea and watching her granddaughter with her soon-to-be-husband outside. They were walking hand-in-hand along one of the paths that ran the entire length of the vineyard. She smiled as she saw Thomas reach down to pick a flower and then hand it to Isabella before he pulled her in for a kiss.

She felt Antonio's hands come around her from behind, his breath warm at her neck, which to this day still made her go weak in the knees over how much she loved him. She tilted her head slightly, feeling the slightest bit guilty, as if she'd been caught spying on two young lovers.

"Hello, my darling."

His words were barely a whisper in her ear.

"Hey you." She turned only slightly to brush his lips with a quick kiss before turning back again, feeling one of his hands gently at her waist, the other pulling her hair back so that his lips could nestle into her neck once again.

"Are you spying, my love?"

She didn't turn around but she knew that if she did, he'd have a smile on his face.

"Just look at them, Antonio. They're so much in love, aren't they? And they're good kids. They'll have a happy life together."

"Yes, they will. He adores her. We couldn't have asked for better for our lovely Bella. I know that for a fact. They are lucky to have one another." Antonio turned Lia gently toward him, as it was his turn now to kiss her on the lips. "Just as we are lucky every day for having found one another again. My dear, if it is possible, I am even more in love with you today than yesterday or the day before."

Lia kissed him back, feeling emotional all of a sudden and unable to hold back a few tears. "Oh, you Italian men—always knowing exactly the most romantic things to say to an emotional woman." She laughed and Antonio laughed with her.

"But you don't doubt me, my love." He winked at her and she kissed him again quickly.

"No, I never doubt you." She sighed without meaning to and then hoped that Antonio hadn't noticed.

"Are you okay, darling? Are you tired?"

"I'm okay. I've just had a little nap actually."

"And how did everything go today—with the others? Did you have a talk with Bella?"

Lia turned to look into his eyes. "I've decided not to tell her—not until after the wedding. I don't want her to worry and I know that she will." She searched his face for reassurance that her decision was a sound one. She knew how he felt about keeping secrets, and for good reason. It was something that they'd vowed not to do in their marriage, and Lia had tried very hard to be honest and upfront in her relationships.

"Are you sure, honey? You could just tell her the truth."

Antonio went quiet and Lia had to turn to see the look on his face that would tell her what he might be thinking. "What? What is it?"

"It's not the same, you know—as Arianna. You're going to be okay. The doctor says there's no reason not to believe that.

We caught it so early and the treatment seems to have done its job."

"Oh, I know honey. Just still—I don't want her to have any thoughts that aren't beautiful and magical during this time. I don't want to ruin that for her." She reached out to squeeze Antonio's hand. "Please support me in this. I have the others—Gigi and Blu—and they've been wonderfully helpful the last few months. And I'm really okay—just a little tired, but that's to be expected."

"Honey—"

"And no—I wouldn't have our friends stay anywhere else." Lia laughed lightly. "Don't you worry about me. Everything is just as it should be."

Antonio looked at her for a few seconds before he kissed her again quickly. "Okay. I trust you." He gently turned her around again so that his arms were circling her from behind—enveloping her with the strength of him. He held her tight that way for a few minutes as they both watched out the window in silence.

Sometimes Lia still felt she had to pinch herself—when she caught a glimpse out their expansive windows or she felt Antonio's arms around her the way they were now. How had life turned out to be so good to her? How was it possible that she'd been married to this incredible man for over ten years already?

And the years had been wonderful to them. The villa—their home—had brought so much joy to her life. Not for the vineyard itself—although she loved the passion that Antonio brought to his land and the crops year after year—but for the sense of home that it had brought her. She felt complete peace on their land together, especially when all the rooms were filled with their family and friends.

"What are you thinking about?" Antonio whispered in her ear. "That time I think it was a sigh of contentment that I heard." He laughed and Lia did as well.

"Oh, I was just thinking, for about the millionth time, how wonderfully blissful our life together is." She felt his arms around her tighten just a bit. "How happy you've made me these past years."

"No words could be sweeter, my love. And that goes double for me. I didn't really know happiness until you came back into my life. Everything else after that has just been icing on the cake."

"The cake!" Lia turned around as the realization hit her. "I have to go pick up the cake!"

Antonio laughed. "What cake? And I'll go for you, love. You stay here with our guests."

"Oh, I'd ordered a cake—it's at the bakery down the street from the restaurant—just a little dessert for our family dinner tonight." She looked toward the clock on the wall. "Chase is due here any minute and I've got everything he needs for dinner but the dessert."

Antonio walked across the room to get his keys from the hook on the wall. "I'm going, love. You finish your tea and enjoy some time with your friends before the house gets loud with the girls."

Lia laughed and crossed the room after him to plant a kiss firmly on his lips. "Thank you, sweetheart. I think I will do just that."

SEVEN

Bella laughed with delight as Thomas handed her the flower he'd picked her and then pulled her in close for a long deep kiss. She'd never realized how romantic he was before they'd started their life together as a couple. She had never seen him as romantic when they were younger—with the other girls he'd dated. Thomas told her that he'd been saving all his ideas for her. That every romantic thought in his head had only ever been reserved for his one true love.

She clasped his hand tight as they made their way along the path that led through the vineyard. She loved walking there and especially with Thomas, who loved it as much as she did.

"So, how was your morning with Antonio? You guys were gone early."

"Very good. Always happy to spend time with your grandfather."

"And? You were off on some secret adventure then?" Isabella laughed.

"Yes, in fact, we were." Thomas laughed and leaned in to kiss her on the cheek. "If you call checking out property an adventure."

"Oh, Lia mentioned that he was looking at a neighboring vineyard. You don't think he'd buy it, do you? It seems like he's busy enough here right now."

"No, I don't think so. He just wanted to look at it."

"Well, from what I can see from here, it must be about equally as beautiful—at least the view, anyway."

"You think so?"

Thomas was looking at her thoughtfully as she nodded, the way he sometimes did when he hadn't quite finished a thought.

"Tell me about your morning, Iz." He grinned. "Tell me about the dress fitting."

Isabella smiled just thinking about what it would be like to have Thomas see the dress for the first time, the day of their wedding. "Nope. Not a chance."

"Okay, so maybe not about the actual dress—you know I like to be surprised by you anyway—but how was the morning with the ladies? I know you've been very excited to all be together again, and I can only imagine how happy Blu was to finally get you into that dress."

"Oh, Thomas, it was so nice. And the dress is gorgeous. I can tell you that much."

"Honey, you'd make a potato sack look gorgeous, but I am beyond excited to see you in it."

Isabella laughed. "A potato sack, huh? Well, just so you're not having any ideas about getting out of wearing that handsome tux of yours, it's most certainly going to be a bit more fancy than a potato sack."

Thomas laughed. "So, back to what we were talking about earlier. It sounds like you ladies have a good handle on the final wedding prep items. I think Antonio and I can handle our to-do list when we're back here before the wedding. I do have a few things to set up back in New York—things we need to take care of shortly after we're back. And the realtor called me to confirm our closing date for the Friday after next."

Isabella willed herself to look happier than what she was feeling. The idea of being back in New York suddenly felt very overwhelming to her. She took a breath in before she spoke. "Okay. That all sounds good. Maybe we can cover that to-do list on the plane or something."

"Iz, are you okay with everything? You don't look so happy. I promise this is going to be a team effort. I don't want you to stress about a thing. It's going to be such a nice change for me to be at home with no classes to worry about."

"Oh, I'm not worried about that. You've been great, honey. We'll get it all done. It's just a bit of packing left in my place, and the movers will get most of it."

"So, tell me what you're thinking, please, Iz."

"Oh, you know I get a bit melancholy whenever it's time to say goodbye here. It's funny that I could spend so much of my life not living here around this wonderful family I've inherited, and yet, it feels more like home to me than where I grew up." She'd said the words without thinking about what she was saying or how it might sound to Thomas and now she watched his face carefully, wishing she could take it back.

"I know, Iz. And with good reason."

"Thomas, I don't mean that Connecticut isn't going to be wonderful. It will be, because it will be our home that we're making together." She grabbed his hand and stopped walking to pull him in for a hug. "And I love the new house. I do. And we'll have our vacations here in Italy as always."

Thomas kissed her on the nose. "And you'll be back here soon —for your party, right? Isn't Jemma throwing you a little bash a couple weeks before the wedding."

Isabella nodded and wondered if she should talk to Thomas about possibly coming for the end of the Positano stay with the women. It would be at least a month before the wedding, though, even if she only met up with them at the end of their stay.

Thomas was waiting for her to answer.

She leaned up to kiss him quickly. "Yes, Jemma says she'll be here two full weeks before the wedding."

"And? What are you not telling me?—and why you even think you can keep anything from me at this stage in our relationship is beyond me." Thomas was teasing her, which made her laugh, despite her misgivings over sharing more with him.

"Well, it's just that Blu has apparently rented this house in Positano—you remember how much we loved the Amalfi Coast?"

They'd spent two weeks together last summer driving throughout Italy, exploring all the places they hadn't made it to during previous visits. And it had been one of Isabella's most memorable vacations with Thomas, the days filled with everything she loved—good food, good wine, and long walks with him through the old city squares or admiring the sunsets in coastal views that were beyond any she'd shared with him before.

"Yes, I do remember spending time with you there." Thomas was grinning as he reached over to place a flyaway strand of hair behind Isabella's ear, a gesture she still found completely sweet and endearing. "So, am I to assume that Blu would like you to join her?"

"Well, to be honest, I guess they'd all—Lia and Gigi too—been talking about it as an extended party of sorts with me. Or maybe not party exactly." Isabella laughed. "But just a time for us to all spend together while Blu finishes up the dresses. Of course they know how busy I am the next few weeks with the apartment and the house and everything, but—well, I promised that I'd talk to you about maybe coming back early for their last week or so there."

Thomas had that look on his face that Isabella loved. Sometimes she could feel him looking at her like that, without even having to face him. It was the look that made her feel completely assured of his love for her. And now she waited for him to speak as he took her hand.

"Iz, you could go with them to Positano. I can handle everything back home."

Isabella's heart beat faster as she squeezed his hand tight. "No, I couldn't do that. It's too much for you to do on your own. It's—"

"Yes, you could. And I can handle everything. I have so much more time now. It's not a problem, Iz."

Isabella looked at him carefully. "Really? You wouldn't mind?"

"Will I mind you being away from me for that long? You know I don't like our separations." He winked at her. "But considering what's at the end of the waiting this time—you becoming my bride —yes, if it's what you want, I think it's a good idea."

"Thomas." Isabella hugged him tight as she felt her eyes grow wet with tears. How did she ever get so lucky, to be loved by him?

"I think it's sweet—that they want to give you that time together. They all love you so much, and it sounds like the perfect, stress-free way for you to spend the weeks leading up to our big day."

"The weeks leading up to the rest of my life with the man of my dreams." Isabella kissed him passionately, her heart bursting with love for him. "Thomas, you really are the best." She tilted her head back to look at him "And you're saying that there are no strings attached, nothing that you're going to be expecting down the road?" She was teasing him. There were never strings when it came to Thomas's love for her.

"Oh, I didn't say that at all." He laughed and swatted her gently on the backside as they started walking toward the house. "Now, let's go tell the others that you're staying. And then you have to promise me one full day together before I leave. Maybe I'll book something in Florence and we'll get a driver to bring you back the day I fly."

"Done!" Isabella grinned back at him, and then, as if on cue, took off running toward the house with Thomas keeping pace right beside her.

EIGHT

Isabella looked across the table at Blu as they both started moaning in delight over their pasta at exactly the same time. "What are you so surprised about, Blu? I assume you get this every night."

Chase laughed as he reached around Isabella to place another platter of meat on the table before he found his seat next to Blu. "Unfortunately, I've been pretty busy at the restaurant most nights of the week—so we're missing our home-cooked meals together."

"Hey, Mom and I cook!" Twelve-year-old Kylie elbowed her dad playfully.

"If by cook, you mean frozen pizza and ordering Chinese." Chase laughed. "I'm joking. Bella, did you know that Kylie has actually turned out to be our little French chef in the house?"

"Is that right?" Isabella grinned at the little girl, who always seemed so happy and full of energy.

"Well, it's been one of my areas of focus for camp. And Gabby is learning it too." Kylie looked at the young girl sitting next to her. "But you prefer to cook Italian, right, Gabby? Like your mom?"

Gabriela nodded her head. "Mostly I just like to cook with my mom in the kitchen here."

"Music to my ears." Lia bent down to kiss her daughter on the cheek as she handed the wine she'd been carrying over to Antonio. "Honey, do you want to refill glasses and then let's have a toast, shall we?" Lia sat down between Antonio and Isabella and gave Isabella's hand a quick squeeze. "Any occasion that we're all together like this is cause for celebration. Isn't that right, Gabriela?" she said, grinning at her daughter.

"Yep! Or like Dad always says—any time we're together is an occasion fit for the best bottle from the vineyard." Gabriela laughed and lifted her glass of sparkling cider.

Antonio laughed too, as he stood up and motioned for Lia to join him. With one arm around her and the other raising his glass out in front of him he looked around the table. "We have a lot to be thankful for today. Lia and I are always so grateful to have you here in our home. The vineyard belongs to all of us, and nothing makes us as happy as having you all here."

"And we are so grateful to the two of you for always making us feel so welcome," Richard said with Emily nodding right beside him.

Antonio nodded and continued. "So today I'd like to toast friendship and family and the sweet anticipation of the union of this lovely young couple." He smiled at Isabella and Thomas. "Cheers to you."

They all clinked glasses as Lia and Antonio took their seats to begin passing the platters of food around for second helpings.

As Isabella looked around the table, once again she felt contentment like she'd not known before. There was something about Tuscany and the magic of the vineyard that made any of her worries lessen. She caught Blu's eye across the table and grinned.

"I suppose I have a bit of an announcement." All eyes turned toward her and she looked at Thomas, who nodded before she continued.

Gigi looked back over her shoulder, as she'd just gotten up from the table. "Oh my, do I need to be sitting down for this?"

Isabella laughed, only just then realizing all the thoughts that could be racing through everyone's heads. "Oh, no. And it's nothing that isn't great or in line with our plans. Thomas and I talked about it, and we've decided that I'm going to stay here until the wedding—that is, if it's okay with you two?" She turned toward Lia and Antonio, and Lia was out of her seat coming toward her before she'd even finished the question.

"Are you kidding? That's the best news I've heard all day." Lia bent down to give Isabella a hug. "Well, it would only be better if you're both staying..." She looked at Thomas.

"No. No, of course I'd love to, but I'll go back to New York, pack up the rest of our things, and close on the house. All the while counting the days until this one is back in my arms." Thomas leaned in to kiss Isabella on the cheek. "But if I have to share her, I'm happy that it's with you all."

Gigi and Blu were speaking quietly to one another.

"So does this mean that we're on for our girls' trip to Positano?" Blu asked.

Isabella grinned. "You're on, and I'm really looking forward to it."

Lia lifted her glass. "Cheers to Positano and our Bella."

Isabella lifted her glass and looked around the table at each of the women. "Cheers to the greatest women I've ever known."

NINE

Isabella looked out at the sea as she sipped her coffee. The villa that Blu had found for them in Positano had completely blown away all their expectations. They'd arrived late the night before when it was too dark to see the magnificent scene that Isabella now witnessed before her.

She'd been the first one up and was enjoying the time to herself. The past few weeks had gone by so fast that she hadn't had a moment to properly process all the events that were taking place.

She turned her head slightly to admire the expansive patio that led into the main living area of the villa. The house was located high above the picturesque town of Positano, which Isabella was anxious to explore.

A month. They'd have a whole month together in this beautiful spot.

Isabella still couldn't get over the fact that Thomas had been so agreeable to her staying. Her heart ached a bit just thinking about him. It had been hard to say goodbye—it always was hard to say goodbye to Thomas. She smiled. But they had their whole lives together to look forward to.

She pulled her sweater just a little tighter and reached to get her phone out of her pocket, bringing up the photos of the past two weeks. Thomas had taken her to a sweet B&B he'd found just outside of Florence. They'd spent two full days together there, enjoying hikes and long talks over dinner and wine.

She laughed at the picture on her phone of the two of them after they'd done a short hike together. She was looking hot and tired. Thomas had his typical goofy grin on his face while he pretended to be about to lick her cheek.

Flipping to the next photo, she caught her breath. It was one that she'd snapped of Thomas without his knowing. He was sitting at his computer, looking down at the screen with his eyebrows furrowed just a bit. Isabella knew that look because she'd seen it hundreds of times over the past four years as Thomas pored over his studies, feeling the pressure of impending assignments and exams.

After she'd taken the picture they had talked about what was bothering him. Isabella knew that he'd gotten an email from his father earlier that day about his start date at work being pushed up a few days. She'd reassured him that it wasn't a problem to cut down their long honeymoon a bit, but she could tell that something was still bothering him.

Why he wasn't sharing something with her, she wasn't sure, but she'd learned over the years that sometimes Thomas needed a little space when it came to managing his stress and worries. Eventually he'd come around and share with her, but he was always so guarded about his feelings affecting her in a negative way. She had to appreciate that about him even if it did frustrate her at times.

She shivered slightly. Despite the briskness of the air, it was her favorite time of day. She'd typically be running at this time of day —but not this morning. This morning was about taking a bit of time to relax.

She turned back to her phone and the pictures of her with her mom. Blu had invited Emily to join them in Positano, but Isabella's parents had friends coming to visit them in Spain. Richard had gone ahead while Emily and Isabella grabbed a quick trip to Siena together.

Isabella looked up as she heard the door to the patio slide open.

"Morning, early bird. Mind if I join you out here? I'm dying to see the view," Blu said as she walked across the patio toward her.

"Morning. Yes, please, and the view is spectacular."

Blu sat down across from her and Isabella watched her take in the panoramic scene.

"Wow! Of course, I'd seen the pictures that the realtor had sent me, but really, they don't even begin to do it justice, do they?"

Isabella shook her head. "It would be hard to describe to someone—just the kind of thing that you really do need to see in person." She sighed. "I wish Thomas could come—later, I mean."

"So, that's for sure then. He won't be able to make it when the guys join us?"

"No, he doesn't think he'll have everything finished in time. But it's okay. Maybe I can convince him to add this spot to our secret honeymoon he's planning."

"So you have no ideas where he's taking you? It will be a complete surprise?"

Isabella laughed. "Well, I may have some ideas. I know that's it going to be in Europe. He's told me that much. I have my suspicions that Paris might be on the itinerary. Knowing Thomas, he may be working to recreate some of our favorite memories together."

"Then I suppose a stay in London might make the list too." Blu smiled.

They all knew how much London meant to the couple. Isabella's first trip there had been both difficult and exciting. Having to navigate her relationship with Thomas while he'd dated someone else had been beyond frustrating, but at the end of it all, their unexpected first kiss had more than overshadowed the trying time they'd been through there.

"Yes, that's possible too, I suppose. I don't know. Thomas has been known to surprise me." Isabella giggled.

"Surprises will keep you young and free, Bella darling." Blu grinned and then gestured to Isabella's phone where she'd set it on the table. "Are those pictures of your Siena trip?"

"Oh, yes. It was great. I think Mom had a really good time. I know I sure did. Wanna see?"

Blu nodded, and Isabella thought about how lucky she was that her adoptive parents had been so easily folded into the mix of her birth mother's family. From the moment she'd first spoken to Douglas and then the rest of them, everything had been so smooth and effortless amongst them. They truly had become one very large extended family. Emily and Richard, as well as Isabella's birth father, Lucas and his family, had been welcomed with open arms, and they'd often come to the Tuscan villa to stay even when Isabella wasn't able to make it.

Somehow, Isabella just knew that this was the one thing that would have made Arianna the happiest. She'd learned a lot about love and family over the years and she had her birth mother to thank for that.

She scooted her chair closer to Blu and together they looked through the pictures she'd taken over the past few days, Blu chiming in with fun stories about a recent fashion show she'd been a part of in the same location.

Isabella put her phone back in her pocket and reached over to take Blu's hand. "I can't thank you enough for this—for everything—the dresses, this place, your friendship." She wiped at a tear. "You and Jemma are both so important to me. I really want you to know that."

Blu smiled and reached over to pull her in for a hug. "You, my dear, mean so much to us. And you don't need to thank me but you're welcome. It's my greatest pleasure to be able to make your dress. I only hope that I can do you justice. You're going to be a beautiful bride, Bella." Blu wiped at her own cheek. "And I know what goes for me, goes double for Jemma. She misses you terribly and can't wait to be a part of everything."

Isabella couldn't wait to see her best friend. They'd chatted a few days ago, and Jemma had said that she was really going to try to make it to Positano for their final week there. It all depended on when Tori got back to the orphanage. Isabella couldn't fault her friend for wanting to help Rafael even though Isabella would bet money that he'd been encouraging her to go. Rafael was very sweet and supportive like that. He and Thomas had a lot in common when it came to how they treated the women in their lives.

Isabella smiled at the thought and turned her attention back to Blu. "And I can't wait to see her. Do you know when it is that she thinks she'll be arrive—?"

"Morning, you two." Lia's voice interrupted Isabella's question, as she walked out onto the patio with Gigi directly behind her.

"My, look how lovely it is out here and the weather..." Gigi stretched her arms up toward the sky. "I think I've died and gone to heaven."

They all laughed, and both Lia and Gigi bent down to give quick hugs to Isabella and Blu.

"Blu, can you help me with something—in the kitchen?"

Isabella didn't miss the telltale smile of mischief on Gigi's face as she spoke quietly to Blu.

"Hey, no secrets here." Isabella laughed. "I'm going to guess that this has something to do with a lovely breakfast coming soon —maybe those scones I can already smell from here."

Gigi laughed as Blu got up from the table, grinning ear-to-ear herself.

"Well, let's just go see what we can do about breakfast then, shall we?"

Isabella and Lia scooted their chairs close together as they

49

sipped their coffees. Within minutes of Gigi and Blu's leaving the patio, Isabella heard the sound of the patio door opening again.

"That was fast! And great, because I'm starv—" Isabella nearly dropped her coffee when she turned toward the door. "Jem!"

TEN

Jemma loved the look of surprise that she saw on her best friend's face as Isabella ran across the patio to hug her. It had been difficult keeping the secret from her, especially when they'd last video-chatted a few days ago. But now it was all worth it.

"Jem!" Isabella hugged her tight. "What are you doing here and why didn't you tell me you were coming?"

Isabella seemed to be both laughing and crying at the same time, and Jemma found herself having to swipe her hand across her own cheeks to wipe the tears coming now. It had been too long and she'd missed her friend. They had a lot to catch up on. Jemma smiled just thinking about all the news to cover between them, not the least of which would be all of Isabella's feelings about her upcoming nuptials. It would be good to talk about everything in person.

"How are you doing? And I must say you are looking beautiful as ever, particularly with this gorgeous sea as a backdrop."

"Oh, you should talk. You look great, Jem. I feel like I need to pinch myself that you're actually here right now. How did you manage that and—wait—how long are you staying?"

Gigi and Blu joined them on the patio.

"Well?" Blu smiled mischievously as she hugged her daughter. "Are you finally going to tell this poor girl or should I?"

Jemma laughed. "Sorry. Poor Mom—and you all—having to keep the secret. And thank you."

Lia hugged Isabella to her. "No worries. I'm sure it was worth the surprise, wasn't it, Bella?"

Isabella nodded, still looking a bit shocked. "Yes, it certainly is worth it." She laughed. "Now is someone going to tell me how long you're staying—how long I get to look forward to having you here—or are you all going to just keep me out of the loop?"

"I'm here for good—well, until after the wedding, I mean." Jemma grinned at the expression on Isabella's face.

Yes, it had all been worth surprising Isabella. She and Rafael had gone back and forth about her coming so early. She'd had to convince him that there was nothing to worry about—that she was perfectly capable of taking care of herself while in Italy. She grinned as she thought about the additional secrets to reveal, but there'd be time for that later. First she wanted to hear everything that was going on in her best friend's head.

"I really can't believe it! You have no idea how happy this makes me." Isabella hugged Jemma close once more. "Come sit. You have to tell me absolutely everything."

"You two go have some privacy. We'll finish up in the kitchen," Gigi said as Lia and Blu were already making their way back inside the villa.

"Actually, I'm dying for a little walk. I'm afraid if I sit down, I won't get back up again after that long flight. Bella, what do you think? Are you up for the walk down the hill."

"Ooh, yes. That sounds perfect. Let me just go grab my shoes. Jem, have you seen the house your mom got us?"

"Only what seems to be a very little bit of it. Mom's getting my room ready along with my dress. I guess I'll do a quick fitting when we get back."

"I can't wait to see you in the dress. Honestly, Blu's sketches don't even begin to show how gorgeous it is in real life."

"That's my talented mom for you. She is pretty amazing, that's for sure. Go! I need to move before I lose my motivation." She laughed as Isabella ran through the door.

Jemma followed after her to go into the kitchen, where Gigi had two warm scones wrapped in napkins for them.

"Would you like some coffee before you go?" Gigi said.

"Or here's some fresh orange juice." Blu handed her the beverage and leaned in to kiss her daughter's cheek. "Honey, are you sure you're okay to go out? I'd think that you'd be feeling pretty tired—after your flight."

Jemma tried—unsuccessfully—to stifle a yawn. "Thanks for the juice. I am pretty wiped out, but I'm okay. We won't be gone long." She hugged her mom. "Don't worry about me."

"I always worry about you, my dear—it's a mother's duty." Blu laughed and held out a second glass of orange juice for Isabella, who had just entered the kitchen. "Here you go, sweetheart. A little energy for the hike back up the hill."

Isabella laughed and drank the orange juice down in fast gulps. "Let's go, Jem."

Jemma glanced over at her friend as they began walking, the silence easy between them as they both seemed mesmerized by the beauty that was Positano.

"Wow, it really is so gorgeous here, isn't it? It's just like the pictures I've seen, only a hundred times better and everything I'd imagine a quaint coastal town of Italy to be like."

Isabella nodded her head in agreement. "It is—and made a hundred times better for me because now you're here. Thanks again—so much—for coming. You have no idea what it means to me, Jem. I still don't quite understand how you're getting away for so long—and what's happening with the orphanage? Is everything okay?"

"Oh, yes. Tori arrived about a week ago. Sorry, I so badly wanted to tell you but I knew that once I started talking about all that was going on back home, I'd somehow let it slip about seeing you in only a few days."

Isabella laughed. "Well, I'm sure I'd be the same if I were trying to keep a secret like that from you."

"So, not that it's easy being away from Raf for so long, it's worth it to be here with you during this time—before the both of us are old married women and have no girl time to ourselves."

"Bite your tongue." Isabella laughed. "Thomas is well aware that I still want to be able to get together with my girlfriends—and old married women? Tell me you really don't think that about yourself, Jem!"

They were teasing each other, and Jemma loved it—it was just like all the memories she had of their travels together during that first year after they'd met. Who'd have imagined that the two of them would be such fast friends? And now Jemma could hardly remember a time when she didn't have Isabella to turn to whenever she needed a friend—for the good times and the not-so-good times. Isabella had been there for her through it all. If only she'd had Isabella in her life during her teen-age years. Maybe she wouldn't have wasted so much time. She smiled. She couldn't regret those times either—it was what had brought her and Rafael together.

"Hello? Earth to Jemma." Isabella was giggling as they neared the bottom of the hill, where some little shops and cafes began.

"Sorry. And no—I don't think that. I'm a happily married woman, and Raf and I are going to stay young at heart forever. And he does plan to come himself just as soon as Tori is feeling back on her feet with everything. I don't think he'll be able to stay away for too long. I can't convince him not to worry—not to miss me too much."

Jemma tried to recover from her slip-up, but the look on Isabella's face told her that she'd not succeeded.

Isabella stopped walking to look at her. "Worried? Why would Rafael be worried about you? Jem, you're freaking me out a little bit. What are you not telling me?"

Jemma bit her lip, trying to decide if she could successfully alleviate her friend's concern or if now was really the right time to divulge the rest of her secret. But she wanted the morning to be all about Isabella. She didn't want to take anything away from hearing her friend's excitement about everything that was happening in her own life.

Jemma laughed and reached out to squeeze Isabella's hand. "Oh, I didn't even mean to use the word worried. You know Raf. He just doesn't like for us to be apart for too long. He's so darn romantic, that one."

Isabella laughed, and Jemma thought she seemed satisfied enough with her response. "Hey, Thomas too—I must say—and let's not complain about that any time soon."

"Good point."

"Now, have you had enough walking? Not to be rude, but you are looking a bit tired, Jemma. Shall we pop into one of these cafes for a coffee?"

"Yes, I'm done walking, yes, I'm quite tired, and yes to a coffee —although I'll warn you now that I'm sticking to decaf this morning. I don't want anything to disrupt this much-needed nap I'm going to take when we get back."

"Sounds good too me," Isabella said, and Jemma linked her arm with her best friend's as she said a little prayer in her head that her stomach would settle.

ELEVEN

Blu helped her daughter up the two steps to the makeshift podium she'd set up in her workspace at the villa. The room she'd selected had a magnificent view of the sea, as did all the suites in the villa. Yes, she was going to be very inspired here.

She smiled. She had taken on a lot, but making the dresses for Isabella's wedding was pure fun for her. Aside from Isabella's dress and the two dresses for the bridal party, she'd already finished the ones for herself, Emily, and Lia. Gigi had promised to give her the fitting she needed this week, and she knew that the weeks in Positano would give her all the time she needed to complete the work.

She looked up at Jemma as together they adjusted the bodice of the dress.

"Honey, did you get enough sleep?"

When Isabella and Jemma had arrived back from their walk, Blu had taken one look at Jemma before sending her straight to bed. Now she examined her daughter's face for signs of how she was feeling.

"Yes, I did. Thank you very much. It's hard to sleep with you all out here in this gorgeous house. And I've hardly had a chance to say hello to Gigi and Lia."

Blu turned as they both heard a light knock at the door. "Your call, Jemma. Shall we invite them in to see?" There were obvious issues with the dress that Blu and Jemma both knew needed to be addressed.

Jemma nodded. "Let's do it."

"Come on in—the whole lot of you." Blu laughed as she called out.

Just as soon as she'd spoken, Lia and Gigi were through the door with Isabella calling out from down the hallway that she was coming.

"Oh, Jem! I knew you were going to look gorgeous, but seriously. Do you like it? The color is good for you, yes?" Isabella walked over to touch the satin skirt of the dress. "And Annie's will match. It's really adorable."

Gigi and Lia were nodding their heads and Blu bit her lip to keep from laughing out loud. She could practically see the thoughts swirling in their heads as they eyed Jemma on the pedestal from top to bottom.

Finally, Jemma laughed and caught Blu's eye as she looked toward the women standing around her. "What? We know it needs to be taken out just a bit. Isn't that right, Mom?"

"Mm-hmm." Blu took a pin from between her lips to place it at the hem of Jemma's dress as Isabella reached out to pull the fabric away from Jemma's waist a little.

"Don't worry, Jem. I'm sure it's not a problem. And you look stunning!"

Blu could hardly contain her laughter. Isabella was such a diplomat, not wanting to say the slightest thing to offend her best friend, least of all something that had to do with as delicate a subject as her slight weight gain—which was arguably much more noticeable in the tightly fitted dress than in the clothes Jemma had worn earlier.

Blu winked at her daughter. "Honey, why don't we take a little break?"

Jemma smiled and turned to address all three of the other women in the room. "So, I suppose I may have a little announcement of my own." She moved her hands purposely to her just slightly protruding stomach.

"I knew it!" Gigi almost instantly had her arms around Jemma. "Oh honey, that's so wonderful."

"Jem! How exciting! I knew something was up with you. Yay! I'm going to be an auntie," said Isabella.

"I thought you had a certain glow about you," Lia leaned over to kiss Jemma on the cheek. "Congratulations, sweetheart. This is wonderful news."

"Wait! How far along are you anyway? You sure have been keeping secrets, haven't you?" Isabella laughed.

"I'm sorry. I wanted to tell you—all of you, but Rafael and I decided that it was best to wait until the second trimester and—well, I'm not quite there, but almost. I can't keep it from you—not when we're all here together like this. Mom knows and you all would have known something was up, as I have definitely been feeling more tired these past few weeks."

Isabella was counting on her fingers. "Okay, so you'll be due in the new year?"

"Yes, the due date is early February. And Bella, I have been wondering how this dressing-fitting business is going to go, but Mom assures me that she can alter it even the week before, if I need it."

"Yes, that's right. It's not a problem at all, and you should go along your merry way, keeping my grandchild happy and well-nourished." Blu laughed.

Grandmother. She still could hardly imagine the role, but it did make her happy. Her thoughts flashed to everything that had happened between her and Jemma over the past years. Jemma's learning the truth about their relationship and Linda had nearly caused their entire family to crumble—it had nearly caused Jemma her life at one point. Blu felt her body tremble at the thought of it.

But things had a way of righting themselves—of coming full circle, Chase liked to say.

Linda would help Jemma and Rafael to care for the baby when he or she was born, and Blu could feel the healing that was still taking place after all these years. Their mother deserved their forgiveness and every happiness that being in their lives brought her.

Blu brought her attention back to Isabella and Jemma, who were laughing because Isabella was saying that Jemma could and should eat anything her little heart—and that baby—desired. The dress would be perfect and Jemma was perfect, baby bump and all.

Gigi and Lia walked over to where Blu sat getting her sewing items together. She'd finish later with Jemma, who seemed to be having the sweetest conversation with Isabella in the corner of the room. The two girls had their heads bent over Jemma's phone, and Blu guessed that she was showing Isabella the ultrasound pictures that she'd shown Blu just a few minutes earlier.

"Shall we leave the kids to chat for a bit? I can bring some tea to the sitting area for us," Lia said.

"That sounds great. I'll be right there," said Blu before she turned toward Jemma. "Jemma?"

"Yeah, Mom?"

"Would you like me to help you out of that dress before we go?"

"Oh yes, thanks."

Jemma handed Isabella her phone and came over to the partition that Blu had set up for changing in the suite.

Blu looked Jemma in the eye before she had a chance to turn to be unzipped. "You are glowing, you know. You're positively the most beautiful I've ever seen you."

Jemma's eyes seemed to tear up instantly. She'd warned Blu that she'd become so emotional lately that it was driving her mad, but watching her now, Blu thought it was a good thing.

"Rafael says he can't get enough of me."

Jemma looked down, but not before Blu saw the red flush creep onto her cheeks. She loved how close they'd become, and even more so since Jemma had become a wife and now mother-to-be. She carefully unzipped Jemma's dress, loving the intimacy of the moment between them.

"Chase used to say that about me too—when I was pregnant with Kylie. I remember worrying when I was first pregnant—and I think a lot of women do—it was hard to imagine what he'd think with all the changes."

"I worried about that too—but not anymore. Rafael is so good about reassuring me. And I can just tell—the way he touches my stomach and even talks to our baby..." Jemma laughed. "Mom, he's just really sweet. I didn't think I could love him any more than the day we married, but I do. I really do."

Blu couldn't help it. She wiped her eyes and waited until she was composed enough to speak, admiring the way that Jemma just let her be with her tears, putting her arms around her and hugging her close.

"Oh, honey. I'm just so happy for you—so proud of you."

Jemma tilted her head back to create a little space between them. "Thanks Mom—for everything. If I can be half the mother you've been to me, my child will be doing okay, I think." She laughed. "Now you scoot. Lia and Gigi are waiting for you and I'm sure they have lots to say about the news. I'm going to go fill Bella in on her list of things to be done as my child's favorite auntie—or favorite of two aunties, I should say. Shh. Don't tell Kylie I said that. She'd be devastated."

They both laughed, and Blu tucked her last items away before blowing a kiss to Isabella. As she headed out the door she could hear the two of them laughing and talking in hushed voices, reminiscent of only a few years ago when they'd been young girls introduced for the first time.

She smiled. "Our babies are all grown up, Ari—and you'd be so proud of them." She couldn't keep herself from whispering the words out loud. It was one of those moments when she could have sworn she felt Arianna's presence all around them.

TWELVE

Lia set the tray of tea and cookies down on the table just as Blu entered the room.

"Well, you've been doing a good job with that secret of yours these past weeks," she directed toward Blu, laughing as she spoke. "Gigi and I were just talking about how hard that must have been for you. Well, you knew how happy we were going to be as soon as we heard the news."

"Yes, in fact, I did imagine that you'd both be pretty pleased. I imagine that the two of you are already planning for the little one's first Christmas at the vineyard." Blu laughed.

Lia laughed too, as that was exactly what they'd been discussing before Blu had walked into the room.

Gigi leaned over to hug Blu. "Congratulations, sweetheart. You and Chase must be so excited."

"Yes, we are. It's going to be a whole new chapter, that's for sure. We're already trying to convince the kids to come stay with us in Florence. We've got that great apartment above the garage that we've already started renovating—and Guatemala just seems so far away and—oh, I don't know. I'd feel more comfortable having them here really when the baby is to be born."

"That makes sense to me. And is that something that Jemma and Rafael are open to?" Gigi asked.

"Well, Jemma is, for sure. She says she'd love to live back here with us. Rafael might take a little convincing, but Jemma thinks she just needs to wait until Tori is feeling settled with the handoff at the orphanage. Rafael has been so busy lately with the kids and the other things that needed to be done around the orphanage, that they've hardly had much time to discuss things, let alone a future move."

"And what about Kylie? Does she know that she's going to be aunt?" Lia asked.

"No. Actually Jemma wanted to wait until after she'd told you all—I think for fear of Kylie spilling the beans early. She'll tell her now, I'm sure—either over video or maybe she'll just wait until the kids get here. Kylie will be as surprised as you all were to see Jemma here early."

"Well, there certainly is lots of great news going on around here, isn't there?" Lia glanced down at her ringing phone. "If you'll excuse me. It's Antonio."

Lia left the others chatting and enjoying their tea as she carried her phone out to the patio, where she could speak with Antonio privately. He'd texted her earlier in the day that he had a few things to discuss with her—something he thought she was going to be very happy about.

As she listened to him on the other end of the phone, she could feel her whole body growing lighter and lighter. It was amazing how one could go through all the emotions that she'd been through over the past year. She thanked God every day that she had Antonio by her side through everything. From the moment she'd truly given him her heart all those years ago—after he'd forgiven her for the secrets she'd kept from him—she'd trusted him completely. He would never leave her side and he would always be her best friend in life. It certainly didn't get much better than that.

She smiled as she listened to him now, thinking about the kids and how alike Thomas and Antonio were when it came to the things of the heart. Thomas's devotion to Isabella was clear in that it was her happiness that he always put above his own. He was a fine young man, and Lia hoped that Isabella could let go of any remaining fears and doubts she might have about their future so that she too would know the joy of what it was to truly trust another with her happiness.

Lia couldn't do that for her—for them—and she'd not betray a confidence in order to make things easier for Isabella now. It was something Isabella needed to learn for herself.

Lia brought her attention back to Antonio, who was laughing at her on the other end of the phone.

"Honey, are you okay?"

Lia laughed too. "Yes, sorry. I'm fine. Just thinking about all the good news we're getting around here today."

Jemma had told her that it was fine to start telling the others, so Lia filled Antonio in on the news that they were going to have a baby in the family soon.

"I couldn't be happier for them. That is joyous news for sure. And Jemma is doing well? How wonderful that she could surprise Bella like that. I'm sure she was beside herself when she saw her walk in today."

"That's an understatement. Aside from Jemma's nap earlier, the two have been inseparable. And Jemma is looking very well—maybe a bit more tired than what is normal for her, but we're going to make sure that she gets lots of good rest while she's here."

"That sounds good. I'm glad you all are having such a good time. Honey, I can't believe you've only been gone a day. How is it possible that I already miss you this much?" Antonio laughed, and Lia felt the lump in her throat that she got whenever the magnitude of Antonio's love hit her.

"I miss you too, baby."

"I think you and I might not be able to make it all these days apart. Maybe I can come down and steal you away for just a night?"

Lia grinned. "Yes, I think we could manage that." She let silence fill the moment for a second as she prepared to get off the phone. "I suppose I should get back to the others. Thanks for calling, honey. Thanks for all that good news. You have no idea how much you made my day."

"I can imagine. So you'll tell the others, then? They can keep it a secret, yes? This has really been stressed to me. I don't think anyone would know except for the fact that we don't want our Bella being uncomfortably upset during this time leading up to their big day."

"Yes, I agree, and don't you worry. Apparently we're all doing a pretty good job of keeping secrets around here." Lia laughed lightly as she thought about the unexpected baby news.

"Oh, and speaking of secrets..."

"Antonio."

"Yes, I know, honey, but if it seems like the right time—I think Bella would want to know and I'm just worried that she'll be upset—"

"We'll see."

"OK. I love you."

"I love you too, Antonio. Thanks for calling, honey."

Lia sat for a few more minutes gathering her thoughts and thinking about how everything was going to move forward with this grand plan underway. Her only focus was going to be on Bella and making this time away special for her. As long as she kept that in mind, the rest would work itself out.

When Lia made her way back to the main sitting room she found everyone there chatting except for Isabella. Perfect.

Jemma filled Lia in that she'd just left Isabella to take a call from Thomas, and Lia filled the others in on everything she'd just learned from Antonio.

THIRTEEN

Isabella clicked open her video app as she made her way back to her suite in the villa. She flopped down on the bed as Thomas's face filled her screen.

"Hi, babe. Wow! It's great to see you!" Thomas smiled and Isabella's heart tugged for missing him.

"Hi. I miss you. So much. How's everything going? Are you regretting your decision not to have your master packer by your side helping you with the apartment stuff?"

Thomas had teased her endlessly about how she'd missed her calling in life, because she seemed to have a special knack for fitting things into the moving boxes. It's like a puzzle, she'd said—or a game of Tetris. She grinned at the memory of packing up everything from Thomas's apartment. They'd shared a bottle of wine and had their favorite rock tunes going all night. Finally, just before sunrise, they'd collapsed together on the sofa, the entire contents of the place surrounding them in boxes.

"I'm getting there. Wanna see?"

Isabella nodded her head and watched as Thomas gave her the tour of the apartment.

"You are keeping stuff there too, though, right? I mean, I think it's mostly the stuff that we'd set aside in the dining room that will go to the new place."

"Yeah, that's right. I know it looks a little crazy now, but I'm getting there. Iz, I promise that I have things under control."

"I know you do, babe."

"But enough about packing and other boring topics—I wanna hear what's going on there. How's the place?"

"Oh, Thomas it's so gorgeous. Look." She turned her phone screen so that Thomas was getting the shot of her suite. "And would you believe there are like eight to ten suites like this—I don't even know how many, but plenty. And I'll have to show you the rest of the place later. The view from the patio and garden is spectacular. I really want to come back here with you—maybe on our honeymoon." Isabella grinned, the camera now back on her where she knew Thomas could make out the silly expression on her face.

"Honey?"

"Yes, my love."

"You are letting me plan this surprise honeymoon, correct?"

"Yes. Absolutely! I wouldn't dream of interfering—except, of course, to maybe drop you some hints now and then—because I know that your goal with it all is my blissful happy smiling face."

Isabella was teasing him but she didn't miss the serious expression that crossed his face.

"Thomas, you know I'm joking."

"Iz, your happiness means everything to me. You do know that, don't you? My favorite thing to see is that beautiful smile on those lips."

Thomas's voice grew low, and Isabella could tell that they'd gone beyond the point of teasing now.

"I do know that, Thomas. And I hope I can make you half as happy as you make me. I mean that, babe. Man, I miss you. What are we doing apart right now anyway?" Isabella laughed lightly but suddenly all she wanted was to be back in Thomas's arms. This was what it felt like to love someone so completely—to feel like a part of you is incomplete without the other.

"I miss you too, honey. In fact, I may have to have you turn your video off because I'm not sure that I can stand looking at your lips another second." Thomas laughed lightly.

"Well, we better talk about something nonromantic then, because I'm not ready to let you go just yet." Isabella grinned into the camera. "Is everything good with the house? All systems go?"

Thomas ran his fingers through his hair before responding, something that didn't go unnoticed by Isabella as it was a habit of his when he was feeling nervous about something. "Oh yeah, everything's good. Don't you worry about a thing. Your job right now is to relax and help inspire Blu by being your gorgeous self in that wedding dress."

"Thomas!" Isabella's sudden recollection of news was enough to cause her to drop her questions about what was possibly bothering him. "You're not going to believe all the news I have for you. There's been a lot of surprises going on around here today."

Isabella filled him on her delight about Jemma showing up unexpectedly and then the even bigger news about Jemma and Rafael expecting.

"Oh, wow! They must be so excited! And how wonderful that Jemma could surprise you by being there. I know how happy that must make you, Iz."

Thomas's look changed just slightly in front of the camera.

"Thomas?"

"What?"

"Well, you're just a bit funny today with all the different looks you're throwing my way. You do know by now that I'm an expert at reading your face, don't you?" She laughed lightly. "So what was that just now? What are you thinking?" She dropped her voice just a bit. "Tell me, Thomas."

"Well, if you must know, thinking about Jemma's news makes

me have the thought about our own family—the one we're going to start, I mean."

"One day in the future, you mean?" Isabella winked at him.

They'd had long discussions about having a family and what that looked like for both of them. Thomas had come from a pretty big family and Isabella had been an only child, so at first she had no idea what their magic number was going to be.

They'd both agreed that they did want children—one day in the future, after Thomas was feeling good about his career and they'd done the traveling that they wanted to do yet as a couple. And then had come the moment of truth when they'd each written a number down on a folded piece of paper.

Visions of opening that paper to a number befitting a small sports team caused Isabella slight panic. When they both discovered that their magic number of two children was a match, it had only solidified their talk about timing and what they wanted to accomplish during their first few years together as husband and wife.

Isabella brought her attention back to Thomas on her phone; he'd been telling her that one day he wanted a daughter who looked just like his bride. She smiled.

"Or a young Thomas would be great too, right?"

"As long as he looks like his mother, we'll be doing fine." Thomas laughed.

"Oh, stop. You know how handsome you are." It was Isabella's turn to grow silent.

"What is it?"

"Thomas, you're going to be a great father. And I can't wait to become your wife."

"I can't wait for that day either, Iz. It seems like it's taken us a lifetime to get here—since Bali, I mean. My future wife has the patience of a saint." He laughed but his voice was low again—like he was trying to hold back his emotions just a bit.

"And I'd wait for you all over again—if it meant at the end of it all, I'd be your wife forever."

Isabella couldn't stop the few tears from falling. She'd had these conversations with Thomas before but it felt really important all of a sudden—as he was preparing to close on this house without her by his side. She needed for him to know that everything was fine for her. That she loved him enough to make anything work.

"Why are you crying, Iz?"

"I just miss you. And I—I really hope you know how excited I am about our future together. I know that it hasn't been easy for you these past months—that I haven't been the easiest in regards to the decisions we've been making. It means everything to me— the house—"

"—I do know that, Iz."

"But I know it was a compromise for you—how much easier things would be for you if we were to stay in the city. And the job with your dad—I know these are your decisions to make and I just really want you to know that I support you, Thomas, that I'll always support you."

"I do know that, honey, but thank you. It means a lot to me. And you're—you're not wrong to question my choices when it comes to the whole career thing. I know you just care about me doing something that I'm passionate about. I get that and I appreciate that—more than you probably know, Iz."

Isabella nodded. "Good."

"So if you can just trust me on all of that, I promise you that I will not do wrong by you—that I will listen to you and we'll grow and figure things out together as we go. Fair enough?"

"Fair. And as much as I don't want to say goodbye, I know you have a lot going on today so I should let you go. I love you, Thomas."

"I love you too, Iz."

Isabella clicked off the app and put the phone down next to

her on the bed, contented thoughts about Thomas filling her mind.

Yes, she certainly was living her dream come true life—more so than she ever would have even been able to imagine.

She leaned over to reach for the small box in her bedside table drawer. She'd made the decision before Thomas had left to go back to New York. She'd spread the ashes in two more spots. The first in Positano. And the final remaining ashes would rest under the big tree of their new home in Connecticut—the home she was building with her husband—for a family that would know about the love of a grandmother who had died way too young.

Isabella put the box away and got up from the bed to walk across the room to Arianna's map that she'd hung on one wall as soon as she'd unpacked earlier that day. It was always the first thing she did in a new place—find a good place for the map, and a spot near where she'd sleep to place a small container of Arianna's ashes.

She smiled as she ran her fingers over the places she'd been these past years. What had started as an adventure with Jemma had continued with Thomas by her side. And, much to her surprise, many of the places were spots she'd ended up traveling to alone.

She placed her finger on the spot where Tokyo was located— and marked—on the map. Just this past year, she'd made the trip to Japan on her own—something that she never would have thought possible even a year earlier. It has been something of a full circle moment for her, thinking about how she'd let her fears and her guard down when it came to learning the ins and outs of traveling around a new city by herself.

Along with Arianna's ashes, Isabella always carried her mother's words with her as well. Some of her favorite letters written to her by her mother had been unfolded and folded so many times that she was lucky they were still readable. But she knew those special few by heart now. They were what always gave her the added courage when she needed it, whether she was facing a small challenge or something bigger in her life.

And Tokyo had been a pretty big challenge for Isabella—worthy of being the final destination she'd marked off on Arianna's map.

She smiled as she moved back a step and thought about the accomplishment of it all.

FOURTEEN

Gigi knocked lightly on Isabella's door, waiting for an invitation before entering the room. It was funny how certain moments caused her such a vivid flash of memory. Just now she could have just as easily stepped back in her mind to a time many years ago where she'd stood outside a young Arianna's room, waiting to help her or comfort her as needed.

It still shocked her at times—in only the best of ways—that she'd been so privileged to have such a beautiful relationship with Arianna's own daughter.

"Come in."

Gigi opened the door and walked across the room to where Isabella was standing by one of the far walls in the suite.

"Hi, honey. I just wanted to let you know that Lia says dinner will be ready in about an hour." She looked at the map in front of them and smiled. "The map."

Isabella grinned at her and put her arm around Gigi's waist. "Do you notice anything different, Gi?"

Gigi's eyes scanned the map once again. "Really? You did it, Bella!" She couldn't help the tears from coming as she pulled

Isabella in closer to her. She knew the accomplishment that it was and also what it meant to Isabella. Yes, Arianna would have been well pleased by the challenge her daughter had taken up on her behalf.

"I did. I did do it, didn't I?" Isabella was grinning at her. "I visited every place that Arianna had marked on the map or written about in her journal. It's quite a lot, really—for just over four years, isn't it?"

Gigi laughed. "Yes, it is quite a lot." She was watching Isabella's face carefully. "What is it, Bella?"

"What do you think Arianna would have done after she'd visited all the places on her list? Do you know of any places that she talked about but never got around to marking on the map? I guess now that I'm standing here really taking this in with you, I'm wondering what the next part of the journey should be—what Arianna would have wanted it to be, I mean."

Gigi reached out to smooth Isabella's hair back from her face. "Bella, let's sit for a minute, yes?"

They sat down on the small sofa and chair just opposite where the map hung. Gigi leaned forward, close enough to take Isabella's hands in her own. "Ari did have a big dream to travel the world, that's for sure. But Ari had other dreams too. You've read her letters and the journals. You know what you shared with me about how Ari wanted you to find love?"

Isabella nodded her head.

"Well, had Arianna not gotten sick, I'm pretty sure that this would have been a big dream of hers too—to settle down with a man who loved her—to build a home together. As much as that girl wanted to travel, she also really loved where she lived with the view of that magnificent bridge. It was special to her there, despite all of the hard things that happened. And in the end, it was the only place she wanted to be—surrounded there by all of us who loved her so much."

Gigi grew silent for a moment as she reached out to wipe away the wetness under Isabella's eyes.

"That's what I think Arianna would want for you—the next part of your journey, Bella. But for sure, I think the important thing is that this is your story—your love story with the man of your dreams. And will there be more travel for you and Thomas? Knowing you two, I'd guess that you'd be adding a lot of your own markers to this great map of yours and that's fun to do but..."

Gigi wanted to be careful with Isabella in this moment. It seemed so important to her—the map and Gigi's words to her about her mother. Gigi knew that, of them all, she was the one who'd spent the most time with Arianna. She and Isabella had had many long chats over the years about everything that Gigi could possibly relay to her about her birth mother.

"But what, Gi?"

She smiled at the young girl, so full of life and hope for the future. "But I think that your marriage to Thomas—your happiness in love and here with your family—those are the things that Arianna most wanted for you. The rest was always just about you finding your way, I think. Even the travel—maybe even especially the travel." Gigi squeezed her hand. "Just look at how much you've changed from that young woman afraid to take her first ride on a plane to come see us."

"Thank goodness for Douglas coming to get me back then." Isabella laughed lightly. "But I would have come, you know. I would have made myself. That's how much I wanted to know you all."

"I do know that, sweetheart."

Isabella seemed to be studying her intently. "Gigi?"

"Yes?"

"Can I ask you something—something kind of personal maybe?"

"Sure, you can ask me anything. Well, you might make an old woman blush, but I'll try."

Isabella laughed. "No, nothing like that—and you are not old."

"Go on then."

"Did you ever feel like you were compromising when you married Douglas? Not in marrying him, of course." She laughed.

"Of course." Gigi laughed too.

"I mean, I'm not sure that I know the whole story but I think when you were first married, you weren't so happy. Is that right?"

Gigi smiled. "That seems like such a long time ago. And yes, you're right. Some probably called me a bit of stinker back then—I probably was a lot for poor Douglas to handle. What am I saying? I nearly drove him mad that first year or so after we married."

"Really?"

"Yes, really." Gigi laughed. "We were coming from two different worlds, you could say. I was used to working—to taking care of people for pretty much my whole adult life. Douglas was getting ready to retire and he wanted to slow down, but with me. And really, he wanted to take care of me. Well, I think you know about how we came to visit Guatemala back then—and find the orphanage?"

"Yes, I love the story." Isabella was smiling at her.

"So really, my dear Bella, you can most definitely attribute that story's playing out the way it did to the undying affection and desire of that husband of mine for a wife who had been in a bit of turmoil back then."

"Well, except that it ended up just as good for Douglas, isn't that right? I mean, I think that he'd probably jumped the gun on that whole retirement idea to begin with."

Gigi laughed. "Yes, I think you might be right about that. You know what I know I'm right about?"

"What's that?"

"I think your Thomas would move mountains to make you happy like that. I see the same love, the same affection in his eyes when he looks at you. We all see that."

Isabella looked down for a moment, something crossing her face quickly, but there just the same.

"What is it? You're not having doubts are you, Bella? About Thomas?"

"Oh, no. Not in the least." She smiled. "I will never have doubts about Thomas. It's just, now I feel like I've been a bit of a stinker myself, I guess. Well, I think things are fine now. We just talked about it, actually. But really, Gi, I was quite adamant about not wanting to settle down back there—back in New York. I feel like I'm done with the city life. I love it when I can breathe fresh air and run in the country."

"And you'll have that in Connecticut, right?"

Isabella smiled. "Yes, I will. So I suppose it's an easy compromise. I mean I do need to support him even if I don't necessarily agree with what he thinks is going to make him happy."

"Like I did with Douglas and his early retirement plans, you mean?" Gigi laughed and then winked at Isabella. "Well, between you and me, my dear, it's quite possible that we do know best when it comes to their happiness. I just think that we need to be willing to sit back a bit and let them steer the boat. You know what I mean?"

Isabella nodded. "Yes, I think I do."

"You just let Thomas take care of you for a bit. I'm pretty sure that he has your best interests at heart."

"I know he does. I shouldn't question that ever. He's always been so good to me. And really, the only thing that should matter is that we're going to be building our future together, regardless of where it is that we call home."

"That's right. And it's to be enjoyed. Every moment."

Isabella reached over to pull Gigi in close for a big hug. "Gigi, I really don't know what I'd do without you in my life." She pulled back slightly to look her in the eye. "I mean that. And I love you."

"I love you too, sweet girl. And you sure do mean everything to me—to all of us. Don't you ever forget that."

"I won't."

Gigi stood. "Now I'm going to go see about helping Lia in the kitchen. Would you care to join me?"

"Yes, I'll be right there after I freshen up a bit."

FIFTEEN

Jemma sat up in her beach chair to take a big bite of the panini that had just been delivered to their table. "Oh, Bella, I am so not exaggerating right now. This one is the best I've had yet."

Isabella laughed beside her, sitting up to take a bite of her own sandwich. "Jem, you say that every single day. And yes, I do agree that they are quite good. And possibly there can be nothing that will ever compare to eating paninis on a beach off the coast of Italy. I will hand that to you for sure."

"Well, the baby seems to love them. That's my excuse and I'm sticking to it!"

Isabella laughed. "Well, you certainly don't need any excuse as far as I'm considered. You really are absolutely glowing."

"Thanks, Bella. And what about you? After only our first week here, you're looking tanned and possibly the most relaxed that I've seen you—maybe ever."

Isabella and Jemma had spoken freely with one another almost from the beginning of their relationship and that bond of sisterhood had only grown stronger over the years. When Jemma had first learned about Isabella's and Thomas's plans for after they were going to be married, Isabella had told her that it was something she'd really been struggling with. Now Jemma watched her friend's face carefully as she spoke."

Isabella grinned. "Yeah, I suppose I am feeling pretty relaxed." She gestured to the water before reaching again for her sandwich. "But who could possibly be stressed here, right?"

"Not us. I could learn to really enjoy this lifestyle." Jemma laughed.

The truth was that they both could afford to live a life of luxury wherever they pleased, but it really wasn't their style— not for either of them. The inheritance that Arianna had left them had done exactly what Arianna had intended, as far as Jemma was concerned. Arianna had wanted the freedom of choice for them, and in that respect, they'd all more than benefited financially. But the greatest gift for Jemma had been Isabella.

"What are you grinning about over there? Still thinking about your food?"

Jemma reached out her hand to touch her friend's arm. 'I'm just thinking about Arianna and how grateful I am to have you in my life. You're the best friend I've ever had, Bella."

"Likewise—well, best girlfriend anyway. I think the men in our lives would beg to differ if we start throwing around best friend awards." Isabella laughed.

"Well, Thomas would have a case, to be sure." Jemma laughed. "So back to what I was wanting to talk to you about..."

"Yes?" Isabella pulled her sunglasses down so that she could make a silly face and wiggle her eyebrows. "What secrets do you need me to divulge?"

Jemma loved it when Isabella's mood was light and playful, and she'd been in the best mood the entire week. The girls had done a lot over the past few days. They'd been shopping for custom-made shoes, hiked a small portion of the Path of the Gods, and yesterday's excursion had them on small boats to check out the

Blue Grotto, something that Jemma did not tire of even after a full afternoon amidst the crystal blue water.

"Well, I was just wondering how you're feeling about everything—about the house and Thomas. You know, everything that had you completely stressed out a few weeks ago. And not that I'm trying to stress you out by thinking about it—that's the last thing I'd want."

"You know, I just feel fine about it. I'm more excited about marrying Thomas than anything else, and there's nothing wrong with the house in Connecticut. It's beautiful and spacious and I know that we're going to be happy there."

"Well, it certainly sounds like you've had a change of heart about it."

"I think it's mainly been about Thomas—about worrying that him working for his dad isn't really what's going to make him happy. I just want him to love what he's doing as much as I love the writing, you know?"

"I do know."

Over the years, as Isabella had gotten more books written and published, she'd developed quite a following, and it was evident that she'd found her calling in life; her fans really connected to her work. Jemma loved how excited Isabella always was whenever she was beginning a new writing project.

"So anyway, I just need to trust him. Thomas will figure that out, and it's not as if his dad wouldn't understand if it's not a fit for him. Thomas's parents are completely supportive. In fact, his mom and I had a conversation recently about this very same topic. She's the one that told me that they'd never had any real expectations about their kids going into the business."

"Well, that certainly makes it easier to go with the flow then, doesn't it? If Thomas discovers that he wants to do something else, it won't be a hard transition or cause any issues with his father."

"That's right—and then there's only the house issue, but it's not like we can't sell the house later if we need to."

"Oh, so what you're really saying is that you want the two of you to strap on your backpacks and travel a bit more." Jemma was teasing Isabella, but she also knew that the wanderlust wasn't gone for her friend.

Isabella laughed. "No, not exactly, although I do hope that we can fit in some more travel. I don't know how to explain it—how I feel about settling down there. I am okay with it. Truly. But it's just hard for me to feel like I'm going to love it there. I am done being a brat about it, though—because that has not been useful to anyone."

Jemma laughed. "You're not being a brat. I totally understand what you mean. It's probably like me with the move to Guatemala. I'm really just there because it's Rafael's home—and he loves what he's doing there or at least he feels an obligation of sorts, which I can totally understand. And it's not that I don't like it. It just doesn't really feel like home to me either."

"Well, now you are going to start your little family. I think that has a lot to do with it, don't you? I mean when it's just us, we're a bit more footloose and fancy-free, so to speak."

"I may have one more little secret for you."

"Jem, what? You're having twins! Go on—I don't know if my heart can take it." Isabella laughed and poked at her friend's arm playfully.

"No, wow—just no to the twins. That would be terrifying. Mom and Chase really want us to come live with them—in the apartment above the garage. She's already started remodeling it and it's actually quite big. They think I'm waiting to talk to Raf, but actually he's already agreed to it."

"Really? That's awesome, Jem! Oh man, I'm jealous now. You all are going to be here and Connecticut feels so far away, doesn't it?"

"It's not so far. And you'll come visit. You'll come when the baby's born—like any good auntie would do."

Isabella laughed. "Yes, of course." Isabella placed her hand gently on Jemma's stomach. "This little nugget is going to get spoiled rotten by us all."

Jemma grinned. She was counting on it—all the love from her crazy extended family pouring out upon her new child. She could hardly wait.

SIXTEEN

Isabella sat outside in the garden as she sipped her coffee. It had become the favorite part of her mornings here. The patio outside the villa was great, but then she'd discovered the garden, which had the most comfortable lounge chairs and flowers that smelled divine. She'd start her mornings with a first cup of coffee outside there—usually by herself, as she seemed to be the first one up these days—followed by a quick run down to the beach.

Once at the beach, she'd head to her favorite cafe, notebook in hand so that she could outline chapters for her current book. And most mornings, at least one of the other women would meet her there for a cup of coffee.

During the afternoon, Blu worked on the dresses, sometimes needing her for a fitting or to look at something or other. It was all coming along nicely, and she was counting down the days until she would become Mrs. Thomas Jordan.

She smiled thinking about her name change. Thomas had been so cute when they'd discussed it, telling her it was completely her decision if she took his name or not—that he understood why she might choose not to make the change. But she wanted to take his name and didn't have the least bit of hesitation about it. In the end, they'd decided that she would become Isabella Dawson Jordan and their future kids would simply have the last name Jordan.

Their future kids. Isabella smiled. Yes, there certainly was a lot to look forward to.

The ringing of her phone on the small table beside her interrupted her thoughts. Thomas. They'd been playing phone tag over the past few days and she knew that he was close to being done with the packing. She clicked the button and waited for Thomas's face to appear.

"Well, aren't you a sight this morning. I'm so sorry about all the missed calls, babe. Jemma and I have been out quite a bit the past few days. The beach here is so gorgeous. I need to send you some pics after we hang up."

"Great, I'm so glad that you're enjoying yourself. I must admit to being slightly jealous. It's been raining here. I'm dying for some sunshine to remind me that it's summer."

"Well, I'm still hopeful that you will finish up early so that you can join us—at least for a few days."

"Me too."

Isabella didn't miss the expression on Thomas's face or his fingers going through his hair.

"Thomas? What's up? Is something wrong?"

"Iz, I have something to tell you."

"What? You're scaring me a little bit." Isabella sat forward in her chair. "Is everyone okay? Your parents?"

"Oh, yes. Not that kind of news. Sorry. It's about the house."

Isabella felt her heart lurch at the tone of his voice. Something bad was coming—something that was going to shake up the little no-stress zone she'd been in. She sighed. "Okay. What is it?"

"It's not going to happen. The owners pulled out."

"What? Can they do that?" Isabella felt her whole body tense.

"Yes, unfortunately. I'm not sure what happened and it really doesn't matter, I suppose. I'm sorry, Iz. We can find another house."

Isabella swallowed. "That one was so perfect—and it took a while to find it."

"I know, honey. I'm sorry."

"It's not your fault." Isabella bit her bottom lip, thinking about how much she should say. "Maybe it's a sign, Thomas—that we're not supposed to be there—in New York or Connecticut after all."

Thomas laughed lightly. "Iz, where do you wanna be, honey?"

Isabella brushed away a tear. She didn't really have an answer to that question. "I dunno. Here is pretty nice right now." She laughed, despite her tears.

"Honey, you want to move to Positano? I don't think that would go over very well with my dad's company. It's not exactly a job I can do virtually—not long-term, anyway."

"I know. Just wishful thinking. And no, I don't want to move to Positano, but I do want you to come here—so I can show you how beautiful it is."

"Iz, don't cry. We'll figure everything out. Okay?"

"But what are we going to do now? After the wedding—well, after our honeymoon, I guess."

"Well, I think we're going to have to stay in the city for a while, babe—until we find another house. Thank goodness we kept your place, huh?"

Isabella's tears increased. She didn't want to live in New York. That was the last thing she wanted. She tried to wipe her tears away, knowing how much Thomas hated to see her cry. And it wasn't his fault. She shook her head. "Thomas, I really don't want to live in New York."

"I know, babe. It won't be for long. I promise."

Isabella took a deep breath, wanting to get off the phone now so she could be alone with her thoughts—alone with the misery of the new situation. "Okay."

"Iz?"

"Yeah?"

"Can you please trust me?"

"You know I do."

"I love you and I want you to be happy, honey. It's all going to work out. I promise."

Isabella smiled. He deserved to know that she really did trust him—that no matter where they lived, she could be happy as long as they were together. She just needed to convince herself of that, and she was sure that she would. She just needed a little time to process the new information.

"I love you too. Thomas?"

"Yeah?"

"Does this mean that you can come here earlier now?"

"Yes, it does. A small consolation, I guess..." He was teasing her.

"Good. I just really want you here with me. I miss you."

"I miss you too, Iz. Now I'm going to get moving around here. I'll get my ticket today—for next week—and I'll send you the details after. Are you going to be okay?"

Isabella nodded and then said goodbye.

But she was not okay. She was not okay at all.

SEVENTEEN

Gigi and Blu made their way down the hill from the villa. Most mornings it was Lia who walked with Gigi, but she'd snuck away for a night with Antonio. Gigi enjoyed the exercise, especially when it ended with a nice coffee meet-up with Isabella. Even thinking about this time ending made her heart ache just a little. Saying goodbye to the kids always had that effect on her. But they still had so much yet to look forward to with the wedding date just around the corner.

Positano had been good for them all. It was times like these with her closest friends that Gigi treasured the most, even if she was missing Douglas quite a lot. The men, along with Kylie and Gabriela, were going to be joining them in a few days. They'd decided to end their "girl time" with a good old-fashioned wedding shower at the villa for Isabella.

Jemma, along with help from the others, had been in full-force planning mode trying to get everything lined up for her best friend. Gigi loved it—every minute of this time with Isabella. And she'd never seen the young girl happier.

"What are you thinking about that has you smiling so widely?" Blu said as they neared the bottom of the hill.

"Oh, I was just thinking how wonderful this time together has been—and how happy I think Isabella is right now."

"It is wonderful. Does it make you think about your own wedding day, Gi?"

"Yes, and to think that we've all celebrated a few together now, haven't we?"

"Nothing could make me happier than to all be together for such a joyous occasion. And I can't even begin to imagine how beautiful it's all going to be at the vineyard. Lia was showing me the pictures the other day—of how everything is going to be set up. Talk about a fairy tale wedding."

"One fit for our princess, that's for sure," Gigi said.

They stepped onto the sidewalk that led to the shops along the beach.

"Did Bella tell you where she would be this morning?"

"She's got a favorite cafe—one we go to nearly every morning. I didn't see a note from her—which she would typically leave if she had another idea—so I assume that's where she'll be."

"What a nice little routine you all have going here. I guess I've been missing out by sleeping in." Blu laughed.

"Well, you've been working late. I've seen your light on. How are the dresses coming, by the way?"

"Very good. I'm nearly done—which reminds me that I need to do one last fitting with each of you today. And I think that will have me close to completion then—well, maybe with the exception of Jemma's. But I'm leaving plenty of room to let hers out over the next few weeks. It does surprise me how much she's starting to show. It seems so early to me."

"She looks absolutely beautiful."

Blu grinned. "Oh, I am not complaining, mind you. Don't think that I can't wait to start sewing some fun maternity clothes for her. She may actually be inspiring me to start a maternity line —or a line of baby clothes, for that matter. That baby is going to be styling." She laughed.

"She's a lucky girl with a fashionista mother, that's for sure." Gigi stopped just outside the cafe. She could see Isabella through the window and from what she could tell, it looked like she was crying.

"What is it?"

"I'm not sure. Let's go in."

Gigi made her way over to the table with Blu close behind her. Not wanting to startle Isabella, she put her hand gently on her back. "Bella? Honey? What's the matter?"

Despite her best efforts not to, Gigi's touch did seem to startle Isabella as she jumped slightly in her chair and then quickly wiped her fingers across her tear-stained cheeks.

"Hey, you two. Have a seat." She motioned for the waitress and then back toward them as they sat down in the chairs across from her. "Two espressos?"

Gigi and Blu nodded and the waitress left to get their order. Gigi reached for Bella's hand across the table. "Bella, I can see that you were crying. What is it? What's wrong? Is everything okay with Thomas, honey?"

Isabella looked like she was really working to hold back tears. Gigi had been around her enough to recognize it on her face. Finally, after it looked like she'd gathered her emotions a bit, she spoke.

"It's the house. I spoke with Thomas this morning and he told me that it wasn't going to happen after all."

Gigi glanced quickly at Blu. They needed to listen and then comfort Bella the best that they could. Thomas wouldn't let her be this upset for long. Gigi had that to count on. And maybe there was a lesson to be learned in all of this. She couldn't help thinking of the conversation she'd had earlier with Isabella about trusting Thomas. She hoped that Isabella could do so now.

"I'm sorry, Bella. Did he say what happened? Or what's going to happen now?" Blu asked.

"Well, he doesn't know much. But the reality is that we'll be staying in my apartment—in the city—until we find something. Who knows how long that will be, though? It's just so frustrating. I was really looking forward to getting out of the city, you know?" She looked over at Gigi. "Oh, boy. It really sounds like I've got that spoiled brat thing going again, huh?" She laughed, but only slightly, as she wiped a fresh tear away. "I'm going to be okay. I know I will be. I'm just processing the new information."

"It's understandable, I think," Blu said.

Gigi smiled at her. "And you're not being a spoiled brat. Like you said, you're just now processing that you two have a new plan for after the honeymoon. Now if you were to carry on, letting this affect your wedding, my dear—well, then I might have to scold you a bit."

Isabella squeezed Gigi's hand. "Point taken. And thank you for that. Guess what, though? There does appear to be a silver lining, which is that Thomas is coming early—here to Positano—after all. That makes me very happy, as I'm missing him something fierce."

"That is very good news indeed," Blu said. "I've definitely been enjoying our girl time together, but I think we'd all be kidding ourselves if we weren't missing our men at least just a bit. I know Chase is really looking forward to it and I do miss Kylie and Gabby too."

"So that is very good news. Thomas will come and you two will talk about your magical future together. You'll see, Bella. I predict that the house falling through is not going to be such a bad thing after all," Gigi said.

The waitress came back to the table with their coffees and Isabella ordered some pastries for them.

"So enough crying for today. I'm really glad you two joined me this morning. You seem to have a way of making everything better. Oh, and I've had a great new brainstorm for a book this morning, believe it or not—right in the middle of my meltdown." Isabella laughed.

"Well, I think there is a saying about heartbreak and creativity, isn't there?" Blu said. "Well, not that this is heartbreak exactly, but you know that. You have Thomas. He's going to make things right for you, Bella. I think we know him well enough by now to know that. Just trust him, sweetheart."

"I do. That seems to be the word of the day. I hate crying in front of Thomas. He gets so bothered when he knows I'm unhappy—and especially now. It's not his fault—not at all. And he's been working so hard to get everything organized on his own."

Isabella stopped to take a deep breath, and Gigi had to smile watching her because she seemed to be doing a very good job of convincing herself. Whatever it took until Thomas got there—until after the wedding, when everything would be happy and glorious—they'd help Isabella to focus on Thomas and the happiness that she was going to feel becoming his wife.

"Thomas has asked me to trust him and I shall. That's what it's all about, isn't it? It's something that I'm still learning, but I *have* come a long way." Isabella laughed.

"Yes, you have, Bella," Blu said.

Gigi smiled. "You're going be just fine, my dear—and an excellent wife to that young man.

EIGHTEEN

Jemma stood on the pedestal in Blu's sewing space while Blu took the waist of the dress out just a bit more than she'd done during the first fitting.

"Good grief, Mom. Do you really think I'm going to get that much bigger in the next week?" Jemma laughed. She couldn't believe that the wedding was coming up in only two weeks. The days had flown by so fast and she'd had such a good time with her family and best friend.

Blu laughed too but she continued working on the dress. "No, I don't think we're going to need it, but it will be easier for me to make it tighter than the other way around—at the last minute, I mean. Honey, you're absolutely glowing, so don't you worry about it at all." Blu stood on her toes to give Jemma a quick kiss on the cheek.

"Okay, if you say so."

"Well, I do say so." Blu winked. "And how are you feeling? You've been pretty busy getting things ready for the shower. You tell us if you need more help with that, okay?"

"I'm fine. Just really appreciating my naps these days. I think I have everything ready for it. Oh, and guess what? I just heard back from Nina that she is going to be able to come tomorrow after all. Bella's going to be so surprised."

"Oh, that's wonderful. Will she be able to stay on with us at the vineyard after? I'm sure Lia has probably invited her to stay."

"Yep, she's all sorted out until just after the wedding."

Jemma and the rest of the family had met Nina for the first time a few years ago and since then, she'd been a regular guest at the vineyard. She'd taken the most amazing photos of the whole family and she'd said without question that she would be the one to do the wedding photos—her gift to Isabella and Thomas.

"Well, things certainly are coming together. Let me show you Annie's dress. Honey, you can step down now. Have a seat over there." Blu gestured toward the chair just across from her work area and then lifted Annie's dress out in front of her for Jemma to see.

"Oh, Mom. It's so sweet. Annie's going to love it!"

Jemma was proud of who Blu was as a designer and a mom. When Jemma was younger, she didn't understand her mom's fame as a world-class designer, and during her teen-age years, she'd been too wrapped up in the not-so-good things to appreciate any of what her mother had done for her—or what Jemma had put her and Chase through. But now, as an adult, she couldn't imagine life without regular phone calls with Blu and the real closeness that had developed between them over the years.

Jemma walked over to sit down in the chair next to her mother's. "Mom, I have a surprise for you too."

"You do? What is it? I'm going to be a grandma to twins?"

Blu was teasing, and Jemma laughed. "Hey, that's what Isabella said to me. Now, don't you two go jinxing me into having twins. I'm not at all sure that we'd be able to handle that."

"Of course you would. So what is it—my surprise?"

"Well, you know how I've been telling you that Raf and I haven't had a chance yet to discuss the possibility of moving in with you guys—above the garage, I mean, of course."

"Yes? And of course." Blu grinned. "Please make my day and tell me that you're coming?"

Jemma nodded and placed her hands over her stomach. "We are. Raf says that there's no reason we can't start raising this little one in Florence. In fact, he wants him—or her—to learn Italian as well as Spanish." Jemma laughed and hugged Blu tight. "I'm so excited about it, Mom. I hope it's really okay with you guys."

"Are you kidding? This is the best news ever. Do you have any idea how happy you are going to make a certain little girl?"

Jemma laughed. She'd had a long video chat with Kylie a week ago, filling her in on the news that she was going to be an aunt. Kylie had been beyond excited and was already begging to be able to babysit when they came to visit. She told Jemma that she was going to immediately sign up for the babysitter's class being offered at her school.

"Well, I guess we won't have any issues finding babysitters," Jemma said.

"You got that right."

Jemma and Blu looked up at the knock on the open door.

"Ooh, can I see?" Isabella said from the doorway.

"Sure, come in," Jemma said as she stood up so that Isabella could get the full effect of the dress on her. "I think Mom is planning that something or other is going to happen with this little bit of extra material at my waist."

Blu laughed. "Well, that's one way to put it. Yes, we're just being prepared." She walked over to give each of the girls a hug.

"I'm just going to go speak with Gigi a minute. Bella, can you help her out of the dress, please? It can be hung just over there on the rack."

"Sure thing," Isabella said, turning her attention back to Jemma as Blu left the room.

Jemma could tell just by looking at Isabella that something wasn't right. When Bella had come home earlier that morning from the cafe she'd gone straight to her room with a headache, and

Jemma hadn't yet had a chance to ask the others what might be bothering her.

"What's up? Why do you look so blue today? Where's my happy-go-lucky best friend and bride-to-be?" Jemma reached over to hug Isabella.

"So you haven't talked to anyone yet?"

"No, I was on the phone with Raf all morning and then Mom wanted to get me into the dress. Are you okay? Is everything alright with Thomas?"

"Yeah, everything is fine. Just thrown for a bit of a loop, I guess. Nothing that isn't manageable, and I do feel a lot better after talking to Blu and Gigi this morning."

Isabella told Jemma about the house falling through and her feelings about having to stay in the city for longer. Jemma listened steadfastly and silently prayed that Isabella would just hang on until the wedding—not letting herself get worked up so much so that she wouldn't enjoy it. No one wanted that, especially Thomas.

When Isabella was done retelling what had happened, Jemma hugged her. "I'm sorry, Bella. I know staying in the city isn't something that you were at all prepared to do. But it certainly sounds like Thomas believes it's only temporary, and if I know anything about that man—it's that he will move heaven and earth to make you happy. Right?"

Isabella wasn't crying at all, though Jemma suspected that there'd been tears earlier. She so wanted her friend to enjoy the upcoming party and the surprise of Nina's being able to join them. If she had anything to say about it, the next few days were going to help her friend to forget about anything that was less than wonderful.

Isabella squeezed Jemma's hand. "Yes, you're right. I really am feeling better about it. Being around you all helps me to feel better, that's for sure."

"Well, good, because you have some fun things to look forward to. Are you ready for your shower?"

Isabella grinned. "Oh yes, and I hope you've not gone to too much trouble, Jem—what with your condition and all."

There was her teasing friend again. "Bite your tongue about my condition." Jemma laughed. "Of course I'm going to do my best to throw you a fabulous party—what with being in such a fabulous place and all."

"Oh, you mean like the one I threw for you?"

"Hey, I loved my party at the orphanage. It was absolutely perfect!"

When Jemma had gotten married in Guatemala, the whole family had gone to stay at the orphanage. Jemma and Rafael had decided that it made the most sense, being the place where they'd first met. A local pastor had come in from a neighboring village to perform the ceremony, and the children had been so excited to take part in the whole event—wedding shower, ceremony and a big party afterward that seemed to go on for days.

Isabella leaned over to kiss her on the cheek. "It was perfect. Everything about your big day was perfect, Jem."

"Just as yours is going to be too. Now what do you say about getting this dress off me and heading to the beach?"

Isabella looked at her watch and grinned. "Well, it is almost panini o'clock."

"You got that right."

As if on cue, Jemma's stomach grumbled loud enough that they both heard it, sending them into fits of giggles as she rushed behind the partition to change into her beach clothes.

NINETEEN

It had been a long day by the time Lia got back to the villa. Antonio had come down the night before, picking her up just before dinner to whisk her off to the town of Amalfi. She had to appreciate the fact that he'd gone through so much effort to spend one night and day with her, she really was missing him more than she would have imagined. He felt the same way about her; it wasn't often that they spent a night apart, let alone a few weeks.

They'd had a wonderful romantic time together, enjoying one another's company, great food, and great wine. Antonio had filled her in on everything that was happening at the vineyard since she'd been away and Gigi had called her earlier in the day to let her know what had transpired with Isabella since she'd been gone. Gigi said everything was fine, but Lia would feel better when she saw it in her granddaughter's eyes for herself.

When she'd come in, Gigi and Blu had been in the kitchen and they'd told her that the girls were upstairs. Isabella had said something about going to write and Jemma might have already gone to bed. Lia poured two small glasses of wine and made her way to Isabella's suite.

"Knock knock," she said outside the door, her mouth close to where it opened in the hopes that Isabella could hear her. "Bella, darling. I come bearing gifts if you can open the door for me, please."

"Be right there, Lia."

A few seconds later the door opened. "Ooh, what's the occasion?" Isabella said, taking one of the glasses out of Lia's hands. "And perfect timing. I'm just at a good stopping point."

"How's your book coming along? We haven't even had a chance to talk about it, but of course you know that I'll be dying to read it."

Lia was one of the few people that Isabella allowed to read her books before they went to her editor. She'd told Lia to be completely honest with her—to rip it to pieces if she had to for the sake of making it better. And Lia was honest with her. She always had been.

Isabella led Lia to the sitting area in one corner of her suite. "Oh, I guess it's getting there. Still early stages but I'm really excited about this book. And how was your time with Antonio? You look like a woman who's enjoyed a night away with her love." Isabella laughed lightly and took a sip of her wine.

"It was divine. Amalfi is such a sweet place—the whole coast, really. If you have time, you and Thomas really should try to make the drive." She saw Isabella's eyes look down toward the floor, a flicker of something. "Honey, Gigi filled me in about the house. I'm really sorry, sweetheart."

"Thank you. I'm feeling better about it now. It was just all a bit of a shock when I first heard. It had taken me so long to wrap my head around in the first place—really settling down there after we're married—so now that it seems we're going to be back in New York for a while yet, I just need to get used to the idea." She sighed and took another sip of her wine as Lia watched her.

Lia reached out to cover her granddaughter's hand with her own. "Honey, it's going to be fine. You and Thomas love one another and really, that's the most important thing. Trust me on that. And you have to keep the lines of communication open. I know you don't like to stress Thomas out when you're feeling bad, but in the long run talking everything through is what will lead you to be even closer together. Take it from someone who knows."

Isabella was watching her intently. Lia had always been very open with her granddaughter. She'd shared everything about Arianna's birth and the silence over the years in regards to Antonio. The hurdle that they'd had to cross when they'd finally reunited had been a big one—one that Lia hadn't been at all sure that they'd recover from. As a result, Lia had become much more honest in her relationships in general, and it was something Antonio encouraged all the time between them, and with those they loved.

"How would you cope if Antonio ever wanted to leave the vineyard? Of course he never would, but would you be able to adjust?"

Lia was quiet for a moment before she answered Isabella. It was a fair question and one she hadn't really considered as it related to Isabella's difficulty. "If it were years ago, I'm not so sure, to be honest. I think, like you, I would be devastated. Maybe I'd cry a lot and try to convince him otherwise." She laughed lightly.

"Like me." Isabella laughed too.

"I guess after you go through some things together, though—some major things—everything else becomes less important. Truly the most important thing is being alongside the man that you love, because you know that you mean everything to one another."

Lia felt her body tensing as they talked. Maybe Antonio was right about her telling Isabella that she'd been sick. She felt like a hypocrite sitting here talking to her about honesty and everything that she and Antonio had been through without filling Isabella in on something very major that had happened in her life this past year. It was wrong. Lia could feel it in her gut.

"I know that you're right, and I'm so thankful that I have such good role models around me when it comes to love and strong marriages. Thank you for that."

After a few moments of silence between them, Isabella reached her hand out to touch Lia on the arm. "What is it? You look like you have something more to say, and it's not like you to hold back with me." She smiled.

"Honey, I didn't intend to tell you this tonight. I—I wanted to wait until after the wedding. I didn't want you to worry, but now... I don't know. I'm not used to keeping secrets from you and it feels wrong to me."

Isabella's brow furrowed. "What is it? Lia, you're scaring me. Tell me."

Lia set her wine down on the small table in front of them and took Isabella's hand in her own again. "Honey, I'm okay. I really am. That's the most important thing for you to know."

"Okay..."

"But almost a year ago when I went to the doctor for a routine exam, they discovered a lump—in my breast. Of course it was very scary at first, but they caught it so early. It was cancer and I've been treated and I'm fully recovered now. There's no reason to think that it will come back. I did have some dark nights, mostly just worrying about the worst-case scenario, but that's what I mean about love being enough, you know? Antonio was such a rock to me during that time. He tried very hard to make it impossible for me to let my mind go there." She finally stopped to catch a breath and take in Isabella, who was wiping at some tears under her eyes.

"And you're sure you're okay now? You're telling me the truth?"

Lia nodded her head. "I am. Truly."

"And why didn't you tell me, Lia? I would have liked to know —to have been there for you."

"I know and I'm sorry, honey. It was something I really struggled with because Antonio didn't want me to keep it a secret from you, but with the wedding planning and all of the happy things happening in your life, I just didn't want you to worry—not when it wasn't necessary. Had the prognosis been more dire, I would have told you. I promise you that."

Isabella leaned forward to hug her. "Well, I'm glad that you're telling me now. And I do wish that I could have been there for you during those times—at least that I could have been there for you to talk to."

"I'm glad too, Bella. And I am sorry. And now that I've completely taken the attention off of your concerns..." She smiled as she lifted her glass of wine out in front of her. "To you, my darling, and this exciting new adventure ahead of you. I know that you and Thomas are going to make one another very happy."

"And to you—and Antonio—for showing us the picture of what a happy marriage looks like."

They clinked glasses and finished their wine in easy silence, a weight lifted for Lia that she hadn't even been aware was there.

TWENTY

Isabella sat across from her friend at her favorite beach cafe. She'd been completely surprised when she'd seen Nina come through the villa doors earlier that day. Jemma had told Isabella weeks ago that it looked like they wouldn't be seeing Nina until the wedding—that she had a photo shoot in Bali that she couldn't get out of. It had been a wonderful surprise to be able to spend the entire day catching up with her friend over good food, wine, and a view that they both agreed rivaled any that they'd enjoyed on their travels.

Isabella and Nina had remained good friends throughout the years ever since they'd met in Greece. Nina had visited her in New York on numerous occasions and Isabella and Thomas had been back to Thailand a few times, which was where Nina had chosen to base herself.

Now Isabella was watching her friend carefully. Something was up. She could spot it a mile away.

"So, you're looking mighty cheerful, young lady." Isabella grinned at Nina as she sipped her drink.

"What's not to be cheerful about? I'm sitting here on a gorgeous beach with my gorgeous friend who's about to enter into wedded bliss." Nina laughed.

"And no words of warning from you?" Isabella was teasing with reference to Nina's more than slightly aloof stance when it came to relationships and matters of the heart. Having met her not so long after a difficult divorce, Isabella tried to understand the perspective that Nina was coming from whenever she spoke about her own policy on dating and marriage in general.

"About you and Thomas? Never! But you know how I feel about the two of you. I'm expecting nothing less than a lifetime of wedded bliss to make me jealous for years to come." She laughed.

"Ever the optimist, you are. And thank you for that. Now I wanna know what it is that you're not telling me. Spill it!"

Nina laughed. "Okay, so I may have met someone myself—someone who's pretty wonderful, actually, and quite possibly we've thrown the word marriage around a few times—just in conversation, of course."

"Really? Do tell." Isabella reached for her friend's hand. "And you have no idea how happy this makes me."

"So, he's a journalist. We met while I was on a press trip in Japan a few months ago—like around four months ago, I guess it's been. He's been living in Tokyo for years. And he's come to visit me already about six times. Yes, so we're pretty smitten with one another, I guess you could say." Nina laughed. "Who would have thought you'd ever hear me utter those words, right?"

"Oh, I'm so happy for you. Nina, invite him to the wedding. We'd love to meet him, of course."

"Oh, thank you for that, but I want to be able to focus on taking your pictures and besides that, he has a business trip during that time anyway. But you'll meet him soon. I'll make sure of it. For now, I shall contemplate love and the idea of marriage through your lovesick eyes. Now tell me everything that's been going on around here. The villa is absolutely spectacular and Positano is one of my favorite places, so coming here was easy once my schedule cleared."

"It is beautiful. I understand why you've talked about it so much. And I'm so glad you're able to be here—for the shower and just to be able to spend a little extra time together."

"So tell me, what is the order of events happening around here? Has it been difficult being away from Thomas these past few weeks?"

Isabella had spoken with Nina shortly after she'd made the decision to stay on in Italy. Nina had always been one to give her good advice—even with the slight chip on her own shoulder when it came to matters of the heart—and she'd empathetically given a big thumbs up to the idea of a girls' pre-wedding trip for Isabella.

"Yes, it has been difficult, but as you'd suggested, I know that it's been really good for me too. Spending this time with Lia and the others has been exactly what I needed. Mom is coming in the morning and I believe Jemma has the festivities starting off with a late afternoon tea in the garden."

"Yes, that's what she told me. It all sounds lovely. I know that she was so happy that she was able to make it out here earlier than you'd expected. Bella, you look really happy. I'm delighted for you and always extremely grateful that we met that fateful day in Santorini."

"The fateful day when you nearly broke your ankle?"

"Thank goodness you were there—for many reasons." Nina laughed. "I count you as one of my best friends. I just want you to know that."

Isabella smiled back at her friend. "I feel the same about you." She thought for a second about how much more time she wanted to spend talking about the situation regarding the house falling through. She'd moved on from it, but if felt like an important thing to discuss with Nina who always had such an interesting outlook on life and a strong belief that everything happened for a reason.

They spent the next hour talking about the house, future

plans, and their mutual love for Italy. As always, Nina offered an interesting perspective to Isabella, one that spoke to allowing her life to be as fluid as possible.

Really, she and Nina couldn't be more opposite in their general way of facing the world. Nina was a complete free spirit, possessing characteristics typical of artistic types. Isabella was creative also, but her life had always been much more structured and organized—or that was the way she'd been before Arianna's gifts had come to her—before Isabella had come to know about her birth mother and the wonderful extended family that would forever change her life.

Nina was trying unsuccessfully to stifle a yawn.

"You should nap, don't you think? You must be exhausted after your flight."

"Well, I was trying to stay up—to get right on local time, but now that you mention the word nap—and now that I've seen that spectacular-looking bed of mine—well, it's starting to sound pretty good, I suppose."

Isabella stood up from the table. "Let's get you back then. Have a short rest, and then I'm pretty sure that Lia has a dinner plan for tonight—something lovely that may or may not include a beautiful sunset."

They'd been enjoying the prettiest skies from their outdoor patio night after night. Most evenings, rather than go out for dinner, they all opted to stay in because everything at the villa was so lovely. Lia and Gigi had even let Isabella and Jemma hire a chef to come in a few nights a week during their stay. It had been important to Isabella that this time away feel like a holiday for all the women, and she knew that Lia did appreciate dining as a guest on occasion.

Everything about Isabella's time in Positano had exceeded her expectations. Now that it was almost time for her shower and then to see Thomas again, it felt like the weeks had flown by.

They made their way outside and began the short hike back up the hill to the villa.

Isabella would see Thomas again in only two days, and in less than a week she would become his wife. She smiled, as she suddenly realized how close she was to all her dreams coming true.

TWENTY-ONE

Blu looked over at Jemma as they worked together to place the tablecloth over the large garden table. Jemma had taken one look at the garden when she'd arrived, declaring it the perfect place for Isabella's wedding shower festivities.

They'd all talked to Isabella about what kind of party she'd like to have and in the end, she and Jemma had decided that it would just be something simple—enjoying the view and their time together. There'd be good food, some wine and, of course, the fun lingerie gifts that the women had picked up for the occasion.

After much debate with Lia, she'd finally agree to let Jemma hire a local restaurant to cater the evening. Jemma had really wanted Lia and Gigi to be able to relax and enjoy the time with Isabella.

Blu stood back a bit, watching Jemma arrange the flowers for the table. Jemma had consulted with a few local florists, but in the end, she'd found her way to the local market where she could pick out and arrange them however she liked. It was something they had in common—a love for color and beauty. It was something that always surprised Blu a little bit, as she discovered the different layers of Jemma's talent.

"Honey, those are beautiful."

"And they smell gorgeous, don't they?" Jemma said. "Hey, Mom? Do you want to see what I made for Bella? Before I wrap it?"

She nodded her head and Jemma walked inside the door, coming back with a small canvas.

Blu knew that Jemma had a secret project going on the balcony off her suite. She'd seen her out there in the early morning hours and heard the instruction that Jemma had given Isabella about the space being off limits.

Jemma turned the canvas around for Blu to see. "What do you think? I wanted something to commemorate our time here together."

The painting was the view from Positano, with the sea stretched out into the horizon and the beach and little shops lining the beach below.

"That's really good, Jemma." Blu ran her fingers along the blue of the sea. "Your work just keeps getting better and better, honey."

"Well, I'm not sure about that, as I've hardly had any time to paint lately."

Blu saw the look of concern pass across her daughter's face. "What is it? What's wrong?"

"Oh, nothing."

"No, not nothing. You know I can tell when something is bothering you." Blu tilted her daughter's chin up just a bit so that she was forced to look Blu in the eye. "What is it?"

"Well, I was just thinking about how hard it's probably going to be after I have the baby. I mean, I have a hard enough time as it is trying to find time to paint. I can only imagine that it's not going to get easier, is it?"

Blu smiled. Jemma had divulged her surprise about their decision to move in above the garage. Blu could probably share a secret or two with Jemma.

"Well, now that you're going to be moving in with us, I think it's safe to say that you are going to have some help with this baby of yours. We will help you, Jemma. You know that, right?"

Jemma smiled. "Yes, I do know that. And thank you. That's a good reminder actually—of how things are going to be a lot different now that we're moving. I can't wait. It will be so good to be back here with you all—especially with the baby coming. I'm sure I'm going to have lots of questions for you."

"Well, I hope that I can help to ease your mind. Now, what I was going to tell you—about your painting. You know we're having the place remodeled—pretty much as we speak."

Jemma nodded her head.

"I'm having them create the most beautiful studio for you— there's lots of light and a gorgeous view. You're going to love it, Jemma." Blu grinned as Jemma hugged her close.

"That sounds amazing. I'm not sure what I ever did to deserve you—both you and Chase—but we sure do appreciate it. I hope you know that."

"We do, sweetheart." Blu smiled. "Oh, and I also wanted to let you know—we're going to talk to Linda—to Mom—at the wedding. Of course, we're going to invite her to come also, and there's plenty of space for her in the main house."

"That's nice. You can try, but to be honest, I have a feeling that she's been quite taken with the kids at the orphanage. She's staying there now, and Tori wrote me to say that she's been such a big help to her."

"Now, that makes me happy to hear. I can only imagine how good it must feel to her—being around the kids."

Jemma was nodding. "Yep, there's a lot of love to go around there. Those kids are hungry for it, and the most loving of any kids I've known." She laughed. "It makes me miss them, just thinking about it."

Blu hugged her one more time before she looked at her watch. "Well, I think Isabella and the others are due back any minute, yes?"

"Wow! Yes, it's almost time to start. How does everything look out here?"

"Like something out of a dream." Blu smiled as she surveyed the garden.

There was quiet classical music playing over the outdoor stereo system, the table look beautiful with big vases of pink and white flowers, and the view of the sea below was visible from every chair around the table.

"You've really done a fantastic job, honey. Now why don't you scoot? Go get ready. I'll mind the fort and not let anyone out here until it's time."

"Thanks, Mom!" Jemma blew her a kiss as she started walking toward the door. "You're the best!"

Blu watched Jemma go and then sat down on one of the chairs, her daughter's words echoing in her mind. Yes, they'd come a long way over the years.

Blu had long since made peace with the tougher times, forgiving Jemma in the part she'd played that had caused such a burden on her heart. Jemma had put them through it, that was for sure. It had seemed as if overnight, she'd gone from being this sweet little girl who loved to play for hours with her mother, to someone who'd just as soon walk out of their lives forever.

Blu smiled as a memory played through her mind. It was a memory of a young Jemma on Chase's shoulders—the first time they'd met Chase, actually—so silly and carefree, so taken with Arianna and their very first stay at the beach house.

"Ari, look at her now. Can you believe your little bean is going to be a mother?" Blu laughed at herself for saying the words out loud, but she couldn't help it. She always had more memories of Arianna when they were all together like this. She thought it was that way for the others as well.

And then a darker memory—a memory of Jemma in the hospital bed—and how close they'd come to losing her and how oblivious the defiant teen girl had been. Yes, things could have turned out so differently for all of them. And one would never even imagine looking at Jemma today, so healthy and full of life, that she'd nearly thrown her life away back then—back when she was too young to even understand what her future could be.

Blu said a little prayer inside her head, as she often did these days, thanking God for Gigi and Douglas in their lives back then to help—thanking God for the bigger plans he'd had for them all.

She smiled as she heard Isabella's voice coming up the driveway.

And she thanked God that a young woman called Arianna had walked into a small bar so many years ago to befriend her and introduce her to a family that would come to mean everything to Blu.

TWENTY-TWO

Isabella took her time getting ready. As of that morning, the house was filled with people. The men had all arrived, including Thomas, and Isabella's reunion with him had been sweeter than any they'd ever had before. They hadn't really had much alone time yet that day, but the next day would be devoted to just the two of them.

Tonight, Antonio had made reservations for their whole crew at one of the best restaurants in town. And Isabella was focused on what she'd wear to dinner—how she wanted to see Thomas's eyes light up when he next saw her.

She thought about the shower that Jemma had hosted for her the night before. It has been so perfect in every way. The garden had been beautiful, the food delicious, and the company around the table was every woman in Isabella's life that meant something wonderful to her.

They'd talked a lot about marriage and asked her a lot of questions about the things she was looking forward to the most. When it came time for the gifts of lingerie, Isabella didn't bat an eye in embarrassment, which surprised even her just a bit.

Everyone around the table knew how special the wedding night was going to be for Isabella. They knew that Thomas would have never seen her in lingerie before the big night. It was special. Everything about the party was bringing her one step closer to that day when they would become man and wife.

All the boxes had been checked off, the traditions upheld, and any nervous jitters talked out.

Isabella looked at the time on her phone and realized that she'd missed a video call from Lucas. They'd been playing phone tag the past few days, and Lucas and the family were due to arrive in Tuscany the next day.

Isabella clicked on his number to call him back. She still had a half hour before it was time to leave to the restaurant. She'd make time for a quick chat.

"Hi. How are you?" She grinned when she saw that the face on the screen was her sister, Annie's.

"Hi, Bella! Bella, we're coming tomorrow. I can't wait to see you and I can't wait to see my dress."

"Hi, sweetie. Oh, You're going to love it. And it looks just like Jemma's. You're going to look like a princess." Isabella saw Lucas and his wife Kate coming up behind Annie to talk.

"Hi, Bella. Can you believe it's almost your big day?" Kate said.

"No, I'm actually almost having to pinch myself to believe it. It seemed so far away and now it's almost getting to be a matter of hours. I can't wait to see you guys."

"Me too. Annie, blow your sister a kiss, and let's let Daddy talk now for a minute." Annie obeyed and Kate gave a final wave as Lucas took over with the phone.

"Hi, honey. Now tell me how you're really doing…"

They both laughed.

"Are you nervous?"

"No. Not really." Isabella smiled. Was she nervous? Maybe she would be the day of the actual wedding, but at the moment she couldn't wait for the day to get there.

"So, we'll see you guys tomorrow night then?"

"Yep, we're going to get into Florence around three; we'll pick up our car and we should be there with you all for one of Lia and Chase's famous dinners."

Isabella laughed. Lucas adored good Italian food and always kept the compliments flowing whenever they stayed at the vineyard, which had become quite a regular occurrence over the past few years.

"Listen, I know how busy it has to be around there and I was the first one to tell Lia not to bother—that we'd happily take everyone out to dinner—"

"Say no more. I know." Isabella laughed. "Lia is definitely the hostess with the mostest. She loves it though."

"Well, honey, I sure am looking forward to seeing you."

"Right before you give me away?" Isabella smiled.

She'd first had a talk with her mother—to see what she thought about having both her father and Lucas walk her down the aisle. Emily had felt so sure that it was the right thing to do that she'd encouraged Isabella to talk to her father, who'd wasted no time in saying that absolutely he would share the honor with Isabella's birth father.

And Lucas had been so sweet, really—always so considerate of not stepping on any toes. It had been that way since the first day that Isabella had met him, and their relationship with one another and the two families had only grown stronger over the years.

Lucas was laughing at her. "Oh, I can't wait, my darling girl."

"Me too. And on that note, I probably should get going, as I have a whole group of people waiting for me here downstairs. Have a great flight tomorrow."

"Thank you. We love you and we'll see you soon."

"Love you too."

Isabella clicked off the phone and walked into the bathroom to give one quick dusting of powder across her cheeks before she made her way downstairs.

She could hear the laughter in the living room long before she was even in the hallway leading up to it. As she got closer, she smiled as she was able to make out bits of the conversation.

"Thomas, she's absolutely going to go wild. I'm sure of it. If you can pull this off..."

It was Jemma's voice that Isabella heard as she rounded the corner and stepped through the doorway into the room, all eyes turning toward her and quite a few nervous glances that told her she'd walked in on a conversation that she wasn't meant to hear.

She looked at Jemma and grinned. "So now am I to understand that everyone knows about our secret honeymoon except for me?"

She walked over to give Thomas a quick kiss on the lips. "Don't worry, I know how you like to surprise me, so I'm not even going to bother trying to get the information out of them."

Thomas grinned and looked around the room. "You heard that here, everyone—straight from her mouth—so I expect there to be no caving."

They all laughed, and Jemma came over to link arms with Isabella as Antonio motioned for them that the cars were there to pick them up.

TWENTY-THREE

Isabella felt Thomas's arms come around her from behind at the same time as she felt his hot breath against her neck. They were alone together hiking one of the paths not far from the villa, and the view was even more breathtaking than the first time Isabella had seen it. She smiled as she had the thought that everything seemed better with Thomas by her side.

Thomas nuzzled her neck with a kiss. "What's that delicious-looking smile for, my love?" He gently turned her face toward his, and the feel of his lips on hers nearly caused her to lose her breath.

She turned her body so that she was tight against him, reaching up to wrap her hands around his neck. This was what she wanted. She wanted Thomas for the rest of her life. She wanted to be his forever. And in this place—this beautiful magical place—she could have been right in the middle of a dream that she never wanted to wake from. But it was real. Thomas kissing her was the most real thing that she'd ever felt.

She laughed as he tickled her side lightly—playfully. She loved the way he teased her. She always had, and it had been the first indication that she'd ever had that he might like her, even though she'd scoffed at the suggestion when her parents had pointed it out to her when they were very young. "Boys always tease the girls that they like, you know?" her father used to say.

And Isabella had thought it was all ridiculous. Of course he liked her. She was his best friend. She didn't even understand what her father meant back then, nor did she care. She only wanted to spend time with the boy who made her laugh—and the boy who just as quickly would dry her tears.

"Iz?"

"Yes, my darling?" She spoke the words into his neck, her breath just barely grazing his ear, which she knew drove him a little crazy.

She felt his arms grow tighter around her and she breathed his scent—fresh soap that she loved mixed with just the slightest hint of sweat from their evening excursion along the path.

"I missed you so much. Do you have any idea how good it feels to be holding you in my arms right now?" He tilted her chin up as he kissed her on the lips and looked deep into her eyes.

"Do you have any idea how good it feels to me to be held in your arms right now, my darling fiancé?" She grinned back at him.

He kissed her on the nose. "And in just a few days, I'll be your husband."

A few days. She still couldn't quite get her head around it. Now that the days in Positano were ending, everything seemed to be moving at hyper-speed. Lia had assured her that Antonio had everything situated back at the vineyard—that all they had to do was return feeling wonderfully rested. But now with her arms around Thomas, she could hardly believe that she was going to be a wife—Thomas's wife—before the week was over.

"Thank you for coming early."

"Wild horses wouldn't keep me away from you a day longer. It was much too long this time. Let's agree not to do that again."

"But look at you now." She smiled.

"Look at me what? Do you take pleasure in my torment?"

"No. Never." She playfully tugged on his lip with her teeth.

"Well, maybe only a little—if it results in you being extra special nice to me when you see me."

"Is that right?" He swatted her playfully on her backside and she reached down, catching his hand in hers and bringing it to her lips.

"Thomas." She felt her voice catch as she spoke. She was serious now.

"Yes, my love." He squeezed her hand.

"I can't wait until I'm really yours—all of me, I mean." She knew she was blushing. She could feel it in her face, but it was important to her that he knew this.

He'd been so patient with her over the years—they'd both been patient—and strong—honoring a commitment that he'd made to her when she told him that she wanted to wait until they were married before they crossed that boundary of intimacy. He'd respected her for it and though it hadn't been easy—not for either of them—they'd done whatever it took to make sure they could keep that promise to one another.

And now, the wait was almost over. Isabella couldn't even speak because of the lump in her throat—the way he was looking at her as she spoke to him about it. It was a look of pure love.

Thomas placed his hands on either side of her face as he gently kissed her. "I can't wait either, Iz. I love you so much for everything you've given me and everything you've yet to share with me. I can't imagine that I could feel any happier when we're together, but I have the feeling that this statement will truly be put to the test."

They both laughed and stepped apart just a bit as if on cue.

Isabella walked over to a small bench just off the path. It was getting close to the time for the sun to set, and they'd need to be heading back soon so as not to be walking along the path in the dark.

Isabella sighed.

"What's wrong, hon?"

"I forgot something."

He looked at her with a question on his face.

"The ashes. I haven't done it yet. I was wondering if maybe you wanted to do it with me this time. It seems kind of fitting. Actually I want to do it at a spot on the beach, so I'll just go by the villa on the way back."

Thomas reached into his pocket and pulled out the small box that contained the ashes.

Isabella smiled. "What?"

He laughed and placed them into her hand. "You always keep them in your bedside table, and you also often forget to bring them with you at the most opportune times."

Isabella laughed. "This may be true. And thank you." She leaned over to kiss him on the cheek.

"You said that this was it, right? The last place?"

"Well, one more after this. I wanted to do it at..."

"At? Where?"

Isabella and Thomas had already said all there was to say about the house falling through. She really didn't want to bring it up any more than necessary. She felt okay about things, but talking about it didn't exactly make her feel better about going back to New York. And she didn't want anything to ruin the lovely time they'd been having.

"What Iz?"

"Oh, I wanted to spread them here and then save the rest for our yard—I was going to save them for the house in Connecticut."

"Oh."

"But it's okay. I'll just hang on to the last of them. Like you said, it won't be long—until we find our home."

"No, it won't be long, Iz." He squeezed her hand and stood up from the bench.

"So you'll come with me then—down to the beach?"

"I can go with you if you want me to, but I kinda think maybe you should do this yourself. It's always been your private time with her—with your birth mother, right?"

Isabella nodded her head. "Yes. But I guess I just thought that with us getting married—maybe it's something I want to share with you now."

"You know what I think?"

"What?"

"I think you should save the last time for us to do together. And I think that if Arianna were alive today, she would have spent every moment with you here in Positano—that it would have been a special time for the two of you."

"And it's a good way for me to honor her—with the ashes here, isn't it?"

Thomas nodded. He understood what the journey—the ashes and the map—had meant to Isabella. And Isabella loved him fiercely for that understanding.

He reached out his hand to pull Isabella up from the bench. "We'll walk down together. I'd prefer you not being on your own now that it's getting dark."

Isabella gave him an exaggerated look of surprise.

Thomas laughed. "Not that you're not capable of being just fine on your own, of course—just that I prefer to be with you at night. Understandable?"

"Yes, understandable." Isabella kissed his cheek as they started to walk down the hill. "And appreciated." She grinned as she picked up the pace a little bit. "There's that shop you were wanting to check out earlier today. It's very close to where I'm going to be. You can probably see me from the window inside." She winked at him. "Will that be to your satisfaction?"

"I think so, yes." He squeezed her hand.

"Thomas?"

"Yes?"

"I love how considerate you are of me. Thank you for that."

"Well, then thank you too—for the same."

"No. It's not the same. Not really. I mean, I love you to pieces and I try to be considerate of you, but somehow it just seems to come more naturally for you. You're just a really good guy, I guess." She laughed and then noticed the serious look on Thomas's face as he stopped suddenly on the sidewalk.

She kissed him, still wanting to keep the mood as light. "What, Thomas?"

"I just really want to love you well, Iz."

She hugged him close so that he wouldn't see the sudden tears in her eyes—tears for the almost overwhelming amount of love that she had for this man who was soon to become her husband.

TWENTY-FOUR

Isabella took a step back from the full-length mirror so she could get a full view of what the dress looked like. Blu had put the last remaining touches on all the dresses that morning and they'd sent the guys off for the day to enjoy a chartered boat ride.

"Oh, Izzy."

Isabella smiled as she turned toward her mother's voice in the doorway.

"What do you think?"

Emily brushed the tears from her face as she came into the room, placing something on the sofa and holding out her arms to Isabella. "Honey, you look so beautiful." Emily turned toward Blu, who was on her way toward the door. "Blu, you've really outdone yourself—with all the dresses. We can't thank you enough. I know how much it means to Isabella."

"It's my pleasure. Truly. I'll just give you two a moment while I let the others know that we're almost finished here. I'm guessing they probably want to see you in it one more time before we pack it up."

"Okay. Thanks, Blu," Isabella said.

Emily moved toward the sofa to retrieve the package she'd set down there.

"Honey, I have something for you—but only if you want to wear it. If you don't want to it's fine, so be honest with me."

"What is it?" Isabella grinned as she walked to where her mom was holding up the item. "Mom! Is that your veil?"

Emily nodded, and Isabella didn't miss the tears in her eyes. "It is. If you like it—if you want to wear it. Well, let's try it on so you can see it, shall we? Do you have your brush?"

Isabella nodded and crossed the room to retrieve the hairbrush that she'd been using earlier while she and Jemma had been experimenting with different hairstyles. She handed it to her mother and took the veil from her hands to hold while Emily brushed her hair.

"Honey, let's have you sit."

Isabella sat there feeling the methodic long strokes of the hairbrush going through her hair as it cascaded around her shoulders. If she were to close her eyes, she could have been six years old again —sitting in the living room by the fireplace while her mother gently brushed the knots out of her hair and her father sat reading a book in his leather recliner.

She didn't even realize the flood of tears was coming until she felt Emily's gentle fingers wiping those tears away.

"I sure do hope those are happy tears."

Isabella sniffled, noticing that Emily was crying also. "They are happy tears. For all the memories you've given me. You and Dad gave me such a good life and now—I just still can hardly believe it, can you, Mom?" She turned around to look Emily in the eyes. "It's funny how life turns out, isn't it?"

"Yes, I suppose it is. Isabella, your father and I are so proud of you and we love you so very much. Nothing has made us happier than to see how fulfilled you seem to be—how you've found your way to what truly makes you happy. It's all we've ever wanted for you."

Isabella nodded. "Mom? Can I ask you something?"

"Sure."

"All of this—our family here in Italy—it really is alright with you and Dad, isn't it? I mean, I never wanted you to feel like I was choosing them over you or anything and—well, I don't think that you do feel that way. But I just want to ask you—to be sure."

Emily hugged her tight. "Oh, honey. We love Lia and Antonio —and everyone. If anything, when they brought you into their family, they brought us too. Your father and I feel completely included—and loved. Oh, there seems to be a lot of love to go around with this lot, doesn't there?"

They both laughed.

"You're not wrong. They do love you—all of them do—and I know that they consider you family just as much as they do me." She turned back around again and handed her mom the headpiece with the veil. "It's really pretty incredible, this very cool family of ours, isn't it?"

Emily took the headpiece and laughed. "It sure is, honey. Now let's see if I can get this into your lovely hair."

Isabella waited while Emily used some pins in her hair and then she felt her hands on her shoulders. "Okay, now you can look."

Isabella stood up to look at herself in the full mirror once again, gasping as she did so. "Oh, it's gorgeous. And it really seems to match the look of my dress too, doesn't it?"

Emily nodded. "I think it does. You look stunning, Izzy. What do you think? It's yours if you want it."

"I think it looks incredible—well, if anyone were asking my opinion, that is."

Isabella and Emily both turned to see Blu, followed by Jemma, Gigi, Lia and Kylie and Gabriela entering the room.

"Oh, Bella, you look just like a princess," Kylie said.

Gabriela ran over and stroked the satin material of her gown. "It's so beautiful." She turned toward Blu. "When I get married one day, will you make me a dress just like Bella's?"

The grown-ups all laughed and Blu reached down to give the little girl a hug. "You bet, honey."

Isabella turned toward the women. "Look what my Mom brought me! Do you love it? It's really pretty, right?"

"It's gorgeous, Bella. And how wonderful," Gigi said.

Lia reached out to fan the veil behind Isabella's head. "I think it's the perfect touch."

"And you're going to look perfect also, my dear. You're so gorgeous." Jemma hugged Isabella and then sat down in the chair opposite her.

Emily walked over to give Isabella a hug, then turned toward Kylie and Gabriela. "Well, I'd promised two girls ice cream at the beach—if it's okay with their moms?"

"Yes! Can we Mom?" Gabriela said.

"Please?" Kylie said, using her best puppy dog eyes on Blu. "I promise we'll eat dinner."

Blu and Lia laughed.

"Go on." Blu said.

"I'm planning for dinner at six tonight. On the early side, since we all need to be up and on the road tomorrow morning," Lia said.

"We'll be here."

"Have fun, girls," Isabella said as she carefully took her headpiece off, then sat down next to Jemma on the sofa.

"How are you feeling? Getting excited? Ooh, how are those vows coming along?"

Isabella had promised herself that she'd finish her wedding vows before leaving Positano. It was something that she and Thomas had agreed on right away—that it was important to them to write their own vows to one another. Thomas swore his were already complete—something which impressed Isabella, as she'd been working on hers since Thomas had left for New York.

"They're coming along." Isabella laughed. "I'm going to finish them tonight."

"Well, I'm sure they'll be brilliant, as is everything you write." Jemma laughed.

"But more importantly they're from your heart. That's what Thomas cares about, I'm sure," Gigi said.

"I could not agree more." Isabella grinned as she looked around at her grandmother and friends seated beside her. Still in her gown, the moment seemed surreal to her. She was getting married in just two days.

Lia reached out to hold her hands. "You are beaming, Bella."

Jemma smiled as she reached inside her handbag to pull out a small bag. "So, Bella, we still have some important wedding details to discuss."

"Really?" Isabella grinned, wondering what her friend had on her mind.

The women had sat around the table earlier in the week to hammer out every detail of the wedding and what still needed to happen. Lia's good friend, Rebecca, had volunteered to be the coordinator for everything that was to happen on the wedding day.

Sofia, the manager of Thyme, was in charge of all the food and the reception, which would also be held at the vineyard.

Antonio had left with all the men earlier that morning to make sure that every last detail was in place.

Yes, it seemed that all they needed to do was arrive at the vineyard to make this wedding become a reality.

Jemma, Lia, Gigi, and Blu looked at one another.

"So, let's not forget tradition amidst all the festivities," Jemma said.

"You have your something old—the gorgeous headpiece from your mother—but I too would like to contribute to the cause." Gigi laughed and handed Isabella a folded handkerchief. "You can keep this in your handbag. It was given to me by my grandmother."

Isabella gently unfolded the beautifully embroidered material. "It's so pretty." She leaned over to kiss Gigi on the cheek. "What a sweet idea. Thank you so much. And I'm sure I might have use for drying a few tears that day."

"I think we'll all be shedding our share of tears. I know I will be," Lia said and then turned on the sofa to face Isabella. "So, you have your something old and your dress—courtesy of our very own talented Blu Foster—is your something new, of course. Here is something I want to loan you for your something borrowed. It's a gift that Antonio gave me on our wedding day, actually." Lia handed her a small box.

The sparkle of the diamonds took Isabella's breath away, as she opened the lid and carefully brought out the delicate bracelet. "Oh, it's beautiful, Lia. I'm so honored to wear it. Thank you." She leaned over to hug her grandmother.

"And last but not least." Jemma winked playfully as she tossed the small bag that she'd been holding in her lap to Isabella. "Your something blue, my dear."

"Should I be afraid?" Isabella grinned as she peeked in the bag and then pulled out a blue garter.

"The obligatory blue garter." Jemma grinned.

Isabella laughed as she reached over to get something out of her own handbag. "Thank you all—so much—not just for these gifts, but for everything—for being with me through all the planning and for enjoying it all as much as I've been enjoying it."

"Of course, honey," Lia said.

"We wouldn't have it any other way," Gigi said and Isabella saw her wipe at her eyes quickly.

"Now, I have something to show you all. It's one more thing I'm adding to my look for the wedding day." Isabella grinned and took the lid off the small box in her lap. She held out the simple silver necklace.

"The locket." Lia smiled and the others were silent as Gigi reached for tissue to dry her tears.

Isabella nodded her head. "I put it on a necklace—because I

wanted to wear it close to my heart." She carefully opened it to reveal two pictures, one tucked on each side.

"Can I see, sweetie?" Lia reached out her hand and Isabella placed the locket open in her palm. "Oh, it's the picture of Ari—from the day she and I were sightseeing in Florence."

"It is. I love that picture of her. It's one of my favorites because the look on her face is one of total happiness." Isabella reached her hand out to Lia's arm. "She must have been so happy with you on that trip."

It was Lia's turn to reach for a tissue. "She was. She was very happy, Bella."

Isabella shifted her weight slightly. "I'm sorry. I really don't want to make everyone sad. That's not my intention."

"Oh no, honey. These are not tears of sadness. Only happy tears. I'm just remembering and knowing how delighted Arianna would be that all of us are here together with you now," Lia said.

"I agree with that," Gigi said. "There is no sadness. We are only celebrating with you, Bella—and possibly getting extremely sentimental in our old age." Gigi laughed.

"Can I see, Lia?" Jemma held out her hand for the necklace. "And that's you right, Bella? Is this the original picture that Ari had in the locket?"

Isabella nodded. "It is." She was thoughtful for a moment.

"Are you okay?" Jemma looked at her and handed back the necklace.

"Yes." Isabella smiled. "I was just thinking that maybe one day I'd be placing a picture of my own daughter in the locket."

Isabella didn't miss the look that passed between Lia and Gigi.

"Well, you know that we are certainly ready for more little ones around the vineyard," Lia said.

"It keeps us young, doesn't it?" Gigi winked.

"Well then, in that case, I'm sure Thomas and I will be getting right on that. We certainly don't want anyone growing old around here." Isabella laughed as she put her new treasure away, feeling completely happy and ready for the next chapter of her life to begin.

TWENTY-FIVE

Lia stood back and watched Isabella with Emily. It was a tender moment between mother and daughter, and Lia couldn't help the draw she felt to observe them from a distance.

Over the years, she and Antonio had come to consider Emily and Richard just as much a part of their family as Isabella was. It had been very important to them that Isabella's parents not feel excluded at all during the process of Lia and Antonio's getting to know their granddaughter, and Emily and Richard had been remarkably supportive and open from the moment Isabella had first connected with her grandparents.

Isabella lifted her hair up and Emily fastened the clasp of the locket around her neck, whispering something in her daughter's ear that made her laugh.

That laugh.

It seemed strange to think it after so much time had passed, but if Lia closed her eyes and listened to Isabella's laugh, she could imagine that when she opened them, it would be Arianna laughing in front of her. Time would have lessened what she remembered about the daughter whom she'd known for such a short time, were it not for Isabella in their lives. Lia was so very grateful for that.

"Isn't she beautiful, my love?"

Lia felt Antonio's arms around her from behind at the same time as she heard his words whispered in her ear. She put her hands over his resting at her waist.

"She's every bit the gorgeous bride that I knew she would be." Lia smiled.

Isabella and Thomas had decided to have their ceremony in the morning, followed by an outdoor lunch and party in the vineyard.

So far, the morning had been perfect. All the women had gathered in one of the bigger guest homes on the property. They'd had mimosas and a light breakfast of fruit and croissants, Lia prepared to have to coax Isabella—who hadn't needed coaxing at all—into eating.

Lia smiled thinking about how calm Isabella had been throughout the weeks leading up to today. There hadn't seemed to be any nerves at all—she only wanted to be Thomas's wife and she'd said that there was nothing to feel nervous about.

"She looks like Arianna, doesn't she?" Antonio said, his words still a whisper in Lia's ear.

Lia nodded against his chest. "I'm glad she decided to wear her hair down. I overheard Thomas tell her once how much he loved it down around her shoulders like that." Lia whispered back.

They'd had a team come in to do all of their make-up and hair. Isabella had sat patiently in the same chair for well over an hour, while her hair was twisted and pulled, until finally she'd stood up and apologized to the hairstylist before pulling the pins out. "I'm sorry. It's lovely. Really. But it just isn't me. Let's leave it down, please."

Lia and Antonio turned just slightly in the doorway to wave at Nina, who was headed their way with her camera. She kissed them each on the cheek and smiled as she moved around the couple to snap some candid shots of Isabella with Emily.

Moments later, she was taking pictures of Lia and Antonio as well and then finally she stopped to chat.

"I've got some great shots already this morning. The way the light is streaming in—it's so beautiful. I can't wait to shoot the bride and groom together out there. Seriously, your vineyard has got to be the most incredible location for a wedding that I've ever seen. Isabella is a lucky bride." She smiled.

"We're the lucky ones—that our granddaughter would allow us such a role in her big event," Antonio said.

"She adores you, you know," Nina said.

Lia smiled as she glanced back toward Isabella, who was now smiling in their direction. "Well, we sure do adore her."

"Shall I get a few pictures of the two of you with Bella? I'll be taking formal shots later, but I always love the candid ones that get snapped pre-wedding—and the brides always seem to love those the most too."

Lia and Antonio nodded and walked over to Isabella, hanging back just a little as it looked like Emily was preparing to leave. She embraced her daughter, and Lia saw Isabella patting at her cheeks with a tissue before she kissed her mom and told her that she'd see her in the vineyard.

"How are you doing, Bella? Can I get you anything, sweetheart?" Lia said.

"No. No thanks, Lia. I'm fine. I just had a pretty emotional talk with my mother. I'm so not prepared to be crying this much. No one told me how emotional this was going to be—pre-wedding, I mean." Isabella laughed. "I've been promised a quick touch-up with my make-up before I go, so I'm trying not to worry about it."

Lia's fingers tightened around the envelope that she held. She was sure that Isabella hadn't shed the last of her tears.

Antonio reached out to give Isabella a big hug. "Well, honey, I'm headed back outside. Not to make you nervous, but the guests are starting to arrive. I just wanted a moment to tell you how beautiful you look—and how taken that young man is going to be when he sees you walking toward him. In fact, I think I better go warn him to bring tissues himself."

Isabella laughed. "Thank you—for everything—both of you. You are making my dreams come true right now. I feel like I'm right in the middle of every fairy tale I've ever read as a child. And I owe that to you two."

Lia hugged Isabella and then kissed Antonio on the cheek. "Honey, I'll be out shortly. Save me a good seat." She laughed, then turned her attention to Isabella. "Bella, can you sit over here on the sofa with me for a minute? Will it be okay—with your dress?"

"Oh, yes. Rebecca says she is going to have them refresh me one more time before I make my way outside." Isabella sat down carefully next to Lia.

Lia smiled at Isabella and then took a deep breath in before she spoke. "My darling granddaughter, I have something for you— something special."

Isabella's eyes widened as her gaze fell to the envelope in Lia's hands. "Okay. What is it?" She whispered the words to Lia.

Lia placed the envelope in Isabella's lap with the writing side up. The handwriting on the outside had faded over the years, but Lia guessed that the letter itself would be typewritten, as so many other of Arianna's letters had been.

Isabella gently picked it up, bringing it closer to her as she read the words out loud. "To my daughter on her wedding day." She looked back up at Lia—the question on her face—with tears already quietly falling down her cheeks. "Lia—when? You've had this the whole time?"

Lia nodded her head.

All those years ago, Arianna had given her clear instructions as the day of her passing grew closer. Lia had completely understood Arianna's desire to make her love known to her daughter. Who better to understand that than Lia?

She'd delivered on everything that she'd promised, and this letter was the last of what Arianna had entrusted to her. Lia could still remember the conversation as if it had happened only yesterday.

She'd been sitting next to Arianna's bed, her chair pushed right up close where she could hear her daughter's quiet voice and hold the hand that had been getting weaker and weaker with each passing day.

Arianna had asked her to get a small packet of sealed envelopes out of her bedside table along with the box of her journals from under the bed. The letters had been carefully labeled, and Arianna knew each journal where a letter would be placed. When she'd finished, a single envelope remained and this one she handed to Lia.

"Give her the journals, please—when you meet her—and she'll find my letters there. But this one—please give it to her on her wedding day. Kiss her and hug her and tell her it's from me—that I would have loved nothing more than to be there with you all celebrating—watching my beautiful daughter walk down the aisle in her gown."

Lia had kept her promise to Arianna over the years, and as she looked at Isabella sitting beside her now, all she could think was what a great privilege it had been. She leaned over to hug and kiss Isabella on the cheek, whispering the words from Arianna. "I'll leave you to read it. Take your time."

Isabella nodded, looking slightly stunned, as Lia got up to make her way outside.

TWENTY-SIX

Isabella sat staring at the envelope for a full minute before she took a deep breath and pulled the folded letter out. Her fingers went to the locket around her neck—Arianna—the locket around her neck was going to help her to feel her mother's presence on the biggest day of her life. But now? Now suddenly her mother's very words to her were sitting in her lap.

Isabella pulled a tissue from the box beside her, noticing how quiet it had become in the guest house. Lia must have asked everyone to give her some time to herself, and Isabella was grateful for that now as she stared at the words in front of her.

My Dearest Daughter,

What a glorious day this is for you. I know how beautiful you must look and how special you must feel. I would bet that you're wearing a gorgeous Blu Foster gown and I hope that you are feeling every bit like the princess you are.

My darling, how I wish I could be there to celebrate with you.

I wish I could have met your husband, for I know he must be extra special to have won your heart, your love, your trust. I hope he makes you laugh, bella—that you smile whenever he is near because you just can't help yourself for the joy he brings to your life.

Isabella laughed as she wiped away a tear. She whispered. "You would love Thomas. He's every bit the man anyone would want for their daughter and he will be a good husband to me."

I trust by now that you've had some adventures, that you're ready to settle down. But don't stop having those adventures. Bring your husband along and encourage him to see the world with eyes wide open. Make your dreams come true for your family, bella. Don't stop believing that you can have it all.

You are embarking on a journey that is foreign to me. I didn't know love—not a romantic lifetime love, anyway. But I can imagine how it would feel to let myself be loved like that. If I had more time, I'd be more open with my heart, but this letter isn't about what I don't have time for. This letter is for the future that is ahead for you. And I'm so very grateful that you are able to read these words today.

"Thank you for writing them—for giving me the chance to hear from you on my wedding day."

Isabella startled herself when she heard her words out loud. She felt an odd sense of calmness, not the intense emotion she'd had the very first time she'd read a letter from her birth mother.

She knew Arianna now. They'd spent a lot of time together over the years—through stories, letters, and the map that shared so much of what her dreams had been with Isabella.

Isabella smiled. They'd been on a journey together, alright.

She brought her attention back to the letter.

. . .

I pray that today is magical and glorious and more wonderful that you could ever imagine. I hope that your wedding night and every day after is spent falling more and more in love with this man you're getting ready to commit the rest of your life to.

You are deserving of every good thing, daughter of mine.

I hope that my words are a pleasant surprise for you today. I hope that they make you smile and that you feel as if I'm there beside you.

And since I can't be there, since all you have of me are these words, I hope that the others are there to celebrate with you—Gigi, Lia, Blu, and Jemma. I feel that they will be. I trust that they are your family now too.

Have a glorious wedding day, my darling. Enjoy every moment, and never for one second forget that I love you more than you could ever imagine.

All my love forever,
  Your Mother,

Arianna Sinclair

Isabella dried her remaining tears with a smile on her face. She noticed Rebecca just outside the window, peering in every so often —probably because it was getting to be about that time.

She folded the letter carefully and put it away in her handbag, which she'd stash until after the wedding.

"I love you too, Arianna."

She stood up and motioned for Rebecca to come in; she did so followed by the make-up artist, Jemma, and one adorable little flower girl, Annie.

"Bella, she's come to touch up your make-up." Annie gestured toward the make-up artist, who was already picking her brushes up from the table nearby. "Rebecca said you were crying. Are you okay? What's wrong?" Annie looked so concerned that Isabella stifled a laugh.

Annie put her hands on her hips. "Bella, do you want to marry Thomas or not?"

This time Isabella burst out laughing. Annie looked so serious —and worried. "Yes, I do. I very much want to marry Thomas, so what do you say we get this show on the road?"

TWENTY-SEVEN

Isabella smiled down at Annie, who was twirling around in circles, delighted with the movement of her dress. Then she looked into the mirror that the hairstylist was handing her.

"Okay, why don't you have a look at the back in the mirror over there?" The hairstylist gave her hair one last fluff and adjusted the headpiece just a bit.

They'd done a quick touch-up to her make-up and hair, and her dress had been freshened up just a bit. It was getting very close to the time that she'd be walking down the aisle to Thomas. She smiled. Now she was beginning to feel some nervous excitement—but more about the excitement than being nervous about getting married.

She smiled at Jemma, who was walking toward her.

"Do you have any idea how beautiful you look right now?" Jemma gave her a big hug. "The dress, your hair, your make-up—it's all gorgeous. And I have something for you—from Thomas, who is looking mighty fine himself, I might add." Jemma winked. "Do you want me to give you a minute? I think we should probably be starting in the next five to ten minutes or so—well, your call, but everyone is seated."

Isabella smiled as she took the card and small box from her friend. "No, stay here with me. I may need your help—if this card is going to cause any tears." She laughed as she opened the envelope and the card inside.

Dearest Isabella (My Izzy, love of my life),

Just a quick note to let you know that my thoughts are consumed with you this morning, my darling. I am a man waiting patiently for his beloved—waiting patiently for you to become my wife.

You, my love, are worth so much more than these simple diamonds. They are but a small token of my love for you and my desire to see you smile every day of our life together.

I love you and I can't wait to be your husband.

Yours forever,
Thomas

P.S. This is present #1 — because I know you like surprises. ;)

Isabella laughed as she read the P.S. and took the tissue that Jemma was handing her.

"Jem, he's so sweet—that husband-to-be of mine." She handed the open card to her best friend as she dabbed at a few tears. "You can read it if you want. And I really need to stop crying now."

She watched as Jemma skimmed the note and Isabella could see her eyes tearing up as well.

"Well, go on. Let's have a look inside that box," Jemma said.

Isabella lifted the lid to reveal two simple diamond stud

earrings, grinning when she saw them—a flash of memory hitting her—a conversation with Thomas about her not being a diamond-wearing kinda girl. It certainly seemed that Thomas was set on changing her mind about that.

"They're perfect—so perfect! I'm going to swap them." She was already handing Jemma the small hoops currently in her ears.

Moments later she stood looking in the mirror at her reflection one last time.

Jemma hugged her. "Ready?"

Isabella nodded as they both turned toward the door where Rebecca had just knocked and then stuck her head in.

"How are you doing girls? Isabella?"

Isabella nodded.

"Jemma, can you come with me please? It's time to get you and Annie ready for your walk. And Bella—Lucas would like to see you if that's okay, and then I think it's go time—whenever you're ready." Rebecca smiled as she opened the door a little wider so that Lucas could enter.

Isabella had had a nice long—and rather emotional—talk with her father over coffee earlier that morning. Again Richard had reassured her that he was pleased to be sharing the honor of walking Isabella down the aisle with her biological father. Richard was the father who'd raised her, but that didn't make Lucas any less of a father to her. She loved that the two men seemed in perfect agreement about that fact.

"Isabella." Lucas's face lit up as he walked through the door toward her and then grabbed her in a big hug. "You look absolutely stunning."

Isabella didn't miss the tears in his eyes. He never held back his emotions with her and it was something that she loved about him. She couldn't help but wonder if it was a side of him that Arianna had ever known—if he'd been as open with her when they were younger.

"Thank you." She kissed him on the cheek and then used one

of the tissues in her hand to wipe off the smudge of lipstick that she'd left behind.

"I just saw Thomas and boy, is he ready to see you."

"Really?" She couldn't help grinning as she thought about Thomas not far from where she'd been all morning, getting ready himself. "Does he seem nervous?"

"No. Well, maybe just a little. I did see him practicing his vows in a corner of the room one or two times."

Isabella laughed. "That reminds me to double-check with Rebecca—to be sure that the pastor has my vows."

"He does. I saw Rebecca handing both sets to him." Lucas reached out to touch her cheek lightly. "So, are you ready?"

"Yes. I think so."

Lucas wiped at the corner of his eye before he reached for her hand. "I just want you to know what an honor it is for me to be able to be walk you down the aisle today. Thank you for that. To think that it was only a few years ago when I first learned about you, and now—now I can't imagine not having you in my life. You've brought such great joy to me since the moment I first met you, Isabella."

Isabella smiled at him. "I feel the same way about you."

"Let's see if I can give you one more hug without messing anything up." Lucas laughed and hugged her close. "I love you."

"I love you too."

Lucas held his arm out for her to take. "Shall we get you to that groom of yours?"

Isabella nodded her head and placed her arm at his elbow. "Yes, please."

TWENTY-EIGHT

Their eyes met as Isabella made her way nearer to Thomas. She didn't miss the grin, the quick brush of his fingers across his eyes. He was looking at her the way that she'd been dreaming of for weeks, months—an entire lifetime, it seemed.

He mouthed the words, "I love you" and she returned the same, her heartbeat quickening just a bit as she finally felt slightly nervous, realizing how it felt to be standing there, her emotions so raw and beautiful among their family and friends.

She stopped at the end of the aisle, with Lucas and her father —now joined by Emily—on either side of her, as they responded to the traditional question of presenting her to the groom. Her father gently lifted the veil back from her face. She kissed both him and Lucas on the cheek before Richard guided her to where Thomas waited to take her hand in his.

Thomas. She was marrying her Thomas today.

Amidst their family, their friends, the soft music that had accompanied her during her walk down the aisle, the beautiful dresses, the incredible backdrop of the vineyard with the sun streaming in—amidst it all, the only thing that mattered to her in this moment was the man standing before her.

She loved Thomas with all her heart and soul. She could hardly stand what with the intense way he was looking at her—the way her heart was beating out of control when his hand took hers.

He leaned in to whisper in her ear. "Iz, you look so beautiful. I can't believe how beautiful you look." He touched her chin lightly, tilting her face just slightly. "Are you okay?"

She nodded and whispered back. "More than okay."

They turned together hand-in-hand to face the pastor.

"Dearly beloved, we are gathered here today..."

And before Isabella knew it, Thomas was standing in front of her with his vows in hand.

She squeezed his hand. "Don't be nervous." She whispered the words and saw him take a deep breath before he smiled at her.

"I, Thomas, take you, Isabella, to be my wife." He paused to look her in the eyes and she tried to keep her composure.

"I promise to honor and respect you. I promise to remain faithful and true to you, to always have your back and to lift you up when you're feeling down. I promise to come to you first, with the good things and the bad, to not be afraid to share my innermost thoughts and feelings with you."

Isabella dabbed her eyes with a tissue as Thomas continued.

He grinned at her. "I promise to be your partner in crime and your biggest fan as we go through life together. I promise to never stop surprising you." He stopped, his voice catching, his eyes weighted with tears. "I promise to always be your best friend. And I promise to love you more and more every day for the rest of our lives."

He stopped to look down and take a breath—to gain his composure before looking her in the eyes again.

"With these words of my heart, Isabella, I bind my life to yours today and for the rest of our lives."

They both took a moment to dry their eyes, Isabella discreetly handing Thomas the tissue he'd asked her to have on hand for him —just in case. She smiled at the thought, both of them sniffling and trying to gain their composure while their love for one another was poured out before God, their family, and friends.

It was Isabella's turn now. With a deep breath, she took the paper that the pastor handed her, looking down for a moment before she looked back into the eyes of the man who loved her so completely.

"I, Isabella, take you, Thomas, to be my husband. I promise to honor and cherish you all the days of our lives. I promise to trust you completely and to come to you when I'm feeling down. I promise to be a safe place for you to lay your head at the end of a difficult day. I promise to support you in your dreams and goals—to be your biggest cheerleader as we go through life together."

Isabella's voice caught as her eyes skimmed the rest of the paper. Taking a deep breath, she felt his hand squeezing hers, his finger reaching out to gently dry the wetness on her face.

She smiled and met his eyes again as she continued. "I promise to trust you with my heart, with our home, and with the future of our family yet to come. I promise to be a good mother to our children and to be a wife who will love you for eternity."

She had to look down momentarily, for the emotion that she saw on Thomas's face caused her to stumble over her words once again. But she was almost done and they were almost husband and wife.

"I promise to always be your best friend, to be loyal and steadfast in my honor to you."

She returned her paper to the pastor so that both of her hands could now be held by her love standing before her.

"With these words of my heart, Thomas—my love, I bind my life to yours today and for the rest of our lives."

Thomas leaned over to kiss her tears away quickly, his hands going to her cheeks.

The pastor laughed, telling them it was not quite time for kisses.

Isabella laughed also, noticing their friends giggling behind them. It was almost time for her to become Thomas's wife.

TWENTY-NINE

Gigi laughed along with everyone else when Thomas jumped the gun with his sweet kisses. She dabbed at her eyes with one hand while she squeezed Douglas's hand tight with the other. Everything about the young couple's vows had been beautiful, and as she watched them in front of her, she didn't think she'd ever seen two young people more in love.

She caught Blu's eye and the two women grinned at one another. Lia, who was sitting just in front of Blu, shrugged her shoulders as she visibly sobbed into a tissue. Gigi's eyes went to Jemma, standing in front of them with her best friend, looking like a princess, herself, in the beautiful gown that Blu had made for her.

The only thing—the only person—missing from the wedding was Arianna, yet it was impossible to feel that she wasn't there. Through the incredible intersection of their lives, Arianna had been the thread that bound them together, a tapestry of love, each woman so different, yet the same. Their friendships had begun amidst unimaginable heartache, yet the years following had been filled with celebration after celebration—and all of it with one another, Arianna never far from their thoughts or times spent together.

Arianna had caused dreams to come true and lives to be changed by the legacy she'd left to each of them. But more than the financial inheritance, had been the legacy of friendship, family, and love.

And standing in front of them, looking every bit like a princess —looking every bit like her mother, Arianna—was their lovely Isabella.

Gigi quieted her swirling thoughts as Douglas's arm came around her and the pastor's words rang out.

"Isabella and Thomas, you have expressed your commitment and love to one another through the promises you have made in front of your family and friends here today. It is with great pleasure that I now pronounce you husband and wife." He smiled at them and then directed his next words to Thomas. "Thomas, you may now kiss your bride."

Gigi could hardly breathe. The moment was so precious.

Unlike Thomas's quick instinctual kisses earlier in the ceremony, this one was deliberate, slow, and lovely.

The bride and groom turned around, hand-in-hand, wide smiles on their faces.

The pastor nodded and smiled. "I present to you Mr. and Mrs. Thomas and Isabella Jordan."

Gigi rose from her seat, crying tears of joy as Isabella and Thomas walked back down the aisle as husband and wife.

THIRTY

Jemma watched Isabella and Thomas as they shared their first dance together as husband and wife. The two were made for one another. Jemma had believed that since the first day Isabella had told her about a best friend named Thomas—a best friend who was *only* a friend, as she'd stressed when Jemma had pressed her during those early days of their friendship.

She giggled as Rafael came up behind her, nuzzling her neck with a kiss, his hands landing on her ever-growing stomach, which he seemed increasingly mesmerized with. "Hi, honey."

"Hi, handsome."

"Do you have any idea how beautiful you look in that dress?" He grinned. "I mean, I thought it was your duty as best friend to the bride not to upstage her but..."

"Oh, stop. Bella looks absolutely breathtaking."

"Yes, she does. And so do you. Shall we join them on the dance floor?" Rafael held his hand out to her.

Jemma took his hand and smiled. "We shall."

Blu watched the couples on the dance floor. Isabella and Thomas looked like something out of a fairy tale. and Jemma and Rafael looked pretty stunning in their own right. She smiled as she admired the way the dresses moved as they danced.

"May I have this dance, my love?"

She turned to give Chase a kiss. They'd been so busy with everything that they'd hardly had a moment to themselves the past few days.

"I'd be honored." She took his hand and he led her out on the dance floor where Blu now noticed Gigi and Douglas. They seemed to be caught up in conversation, Gigi's head back as Douglas swung her around before dipping her rather dramatically.

Blu put her arms around Chase's neck and pulled him close for a kiss. "It was such a beautiful wedding, wasn't it?"

"One of the finest I've seen. I'm so happy for them both. They deserve it."

Blu nodded. "Chase, look."

He followed her eyes to where Jemma and Rafael were dancing. Rafael had placed his hand on Jemma's stomach and she was laughing as she removed it.

"They're going to make great parents."

"And you are going to be a terrific grandmother."

"Oh wow! That sounds so weird—to hear you say that." Blu laughed. "Am I actually ready to be a grandmother?"

"Well, you're going be a really cool grandma anyway. That's for sure," Chase said and kissed her on the lips.

"And yes, I can't wait," Blu said.

Blu's eyes swept across the dance floor, taking in all the couples that were dancing now. "Lia and Antonio look so happy."

"There's a lot to be happy about, I think," Chase said. "They've made it through a rough patch this last year." He nodded in the direction of Isabella and Thomas dancing. "But I have the feeling that this wedding is just the beginning of what's going to be an incredible year ahead."

Blu laughed and kissed him as she thought about all the wonderful changes happening in all their lives. "I think it's going to be an incredible year here for all of us."

THIRTY-ONE

Isabella turned around and waved to all their cheering family and friends before she slid into the waiting limo with Thomas right behind her. Thomas moved toward the front of the passenger compartment to speak with the driver in a quiet voice—giving him their departure information, Isabella suspected.

She still had no idea where they were going on their honeymoon, but the sun hadn't set yet, and it would make the most sense that they'd be going to the airport in Florence.

While Isabella waited for Thomas to finish speaking to the driver, she took some clothes out of the bag she'd brought with her. They'd decided to leave in their wedding clothes and change in the limo en route to the airport.

Isabella felt her face flush thinking about it. Finally, she could change in front of Thomas with no reservations. The unexpected thought thrilled her, and she smiled as the privacy window went up between the driver and them. They hadn't started down the driveway yet, but with the door shut and the windows so darkly tinted, they'd finally be alone as husband and wife—something she'd been looking forward to all day.

Thomas came back to sit beside her, taking the clothes from her hands to put them aside.

"Not yet. I want to kiss you while you're still in that dress—really kiss you, I mean."

He grinned at her and as he took her face in his hands and kissed her so sweetly, Isabella's heart pounded fast, wanting more now than just his sweet kisses. She wanted to be his wife, fully and completely.

"I love you so much, Thomas." She tried to deepen the kiss, but now he gently pulled away.

"Not yet. I want to talk to you. I want to hold my wife's hand and drink in your beauty now that we're finally alone together."

Isabella laughed lightly. "Do you also want to tell me where we're going? Or is that surprise going to last until we get to the airport?"

The car started down the long driveway and Thomas leaned in to kiss her quickly on the lips. "Oh, so you think you know that we're going to the airport, huh?"

"Well, you know me. I am a pretty logical girl." She grinned.

"But"—he interrupted himself to kiss her deeply on the mouth—"the question is, does this undeniably intelligent and logical girl—who happens to be dressed like a princess—also believe in fairy tales coming true?"

Before she could answer him, he placed a small wrapped box in her lap.

She smiled as she sat up from where she'd been leaning against the seat. "Surprise wedding gift number two, I take it?"

Thomas nodded, and Isabella thought he looked as if he might not be able to contain his excitement for her to open the gift.

She lifted the lid and then the tissue paper that was inside to reveal a key. She grinned. "So, I take it that I finally have the key to your heart?"

Thomas kissed her. "I think it's fair to say that you've had my heart for quite a while now, my darling."

Isabella laughed and kissed him back, enjoying their teasing and the way Thomas was looking at her. "Is that so?"

"Most definitely."

"Okay, so the key..." Isabella pulled back just a bit to look at him. "Thomas? Is it—" Her heart was suddenly beating faster, her mind swirling with so many thoughts at once. "The house? We got the house in Connecticut after all?"

Thomas seemed to be enjoying her confusion.

She punched him playfully on the arm. "Thomas, say something. Tell me what this key is for."

He kissed her again and she pushed him away gently.

"No, we didn't get the house in Connecticut, Iz."

"Okay, then what? Thomas, is this a key to a house or are you playing some kind of joke on me?" She wasn't exactly irritated, but she was at the point of really wanting some answers.

"Yes, Iz. It is the key to a house—to our house."

She smiled, letting the words sink in. "You found us a house? Is it in Connecticut? Thomas! Are you going to show me pictures or something? This is an incredible surprise—you have no idea—but I just want to know what I'm thanking you for." Isabella laughed and felt the one annoying weight of the past weeks lift from her shoulders. They didn't have to go back to live in the city. The thought brought her such a sense of relief, that before she knew it, tears were rolling down her cheeks.

"Oh, honey, don't cry." Thomas reached for a tissue and then dried her eyes. "You haven't even seen a picture yet." He laughed lightly.

Isabella sniffled. "I'm just really happy that we're not going to be living in the city." She looked up at him. "Does it have a big yard?"

Thomas nodded his head and leaned back with his phone in his hand. "It does have a yard, a very big yard, in fact. Would you like to see a picture?" He grinned.

"Yes, please."

Isabella looked at the picture Thomas brought up, squinting her eyes a bit as she tried to make out what it was she was looking at. "I don't get it. That kind of looks like the vineyard—like Lia and Antonio's place."

Thomas kissed her and Isabella felt the fresh air and saw the light of dusk coming through the door that had been opened by their driver. It was only in that moment that she'd even realized the car had stopped.

Thomas moved around her to step outside the door of the limo, his body blocking her view to the outside.

"I don't get it. Thomas, where are we?" Isabella felt genuine confusion as she looked at him grinning at her from the doorway.

Thomas reached out his hand toward her. "Come here, my love. Let me show you our new home."

THIRTY-TWO

Isabella stood outside the front door of the large villa with Thomas, their backs to the house as Thomas pointed out the perimeters of the land, his voice rising with the excitement of a man with a passionate plan—a plan for this beautiful vineyard that Isabella could now see went on for miles.

She listened in stunned silence, knowing that when the time came for her to speak, words would betray her. She was so absolutely overcome with emotion for what he'd done. He'd taken the best day of her life—and incredibly—just made it better than anything she could have ever imagined. It *was* her fairy tale come true.

She took a slow breath in of the cool evening air and tried to focus on what Thomas was saying to her. She followed his finger where he pointed, out across the land, now colored with the Tuscan sunset that Isabella had come to love.

"Look. Right over there, you can just see the top of the roof of your grandparents' place." His arms came around her then, his hands finding their way around her waist, his lips nuzzled up against her neck as tears coursed down her cheeks.

"Iz? Honey, do you like your surprise?"

She knew without looking that he was smiling from ear to ear. She knew without speaking that he could sense what it all meant to her—how overcome with emotion she was. She nodded her head against his chest, her senses overwhelmed by everything she was seeing, by the words he was speaking to her about their future —a future that would be lived out here in Tuscany.

She turned around in his arms, her eyes finding his, the tears freely falling down her face as he worked just as quickly to kiss them away.

"Iz? Honey? I sure do hope those are happy tears..."

Isabella laughed and then kissed him on the lips, shocking herself with the intensity of what she was feeling for this man who had just made her every dream come true.

He kissed her back, his fingers touching her cheek and then entangled in her hair.

"Thomas, I love you so much. Do you have any idea how happy you've made me? I really can't believe that you did this— how did you manage—"

He stopped her questions with another kiss and then pulled away slightly to look into her eyes again. "I meant it when I said that your happiness means everything to me. I will spend the rest of our lives together keeping that promise. You do know that, don't you?"

"Yes, but—but what about you? Thomas, I want you to be happy too. Nothing matters to me, if what you want is being sacrificed. I could never live with myself, if I thought that you were giving up—"

"Iz, look at this place." His arms stretched out in front of them and he laughed. "If you only knew...but then again, how could you know?" He winked at her.

She took both of his hands in hers and kissed him sweetly. She couldn't get enough of his kisses. "So what are you saying? Who knew about this little scheme of yours?" She laughed at the silly face he made. "So, basically everyone was in on it?"

"We've got great friends, Iz." Thomas laughed. "But on a serious note, your grandfather has been such a mentor to me. He spoke to me about the vineyard as soon as it came up for sale. You know Antonio...he's promised to help me get it all going and—I don't know—he seems to have a lot of confidence that I can make it work. And I love it, Iz. I really do."

Isabella loved the way Thomas's eyes sparkled brighter when he talked about the vineyard. She was already learning a thing or two about trusting this husband of hers.

Her husband. She grinned as she had the thought.

"Thomas?"

"Yes?"

"Does this mean that we're not going to the airport tonight?"

"Correct. Our official honeymoon will start tomorrow after Lia and the others bring over a fantastic brunch that I know they're very excited about." He kissed her neck and whispered in her ear. "Does that sound okay to you?"

"Mm-hm—well, except for one part of that plan." She kissed him deeply on the mouth, and this time neither of them held back the longing that had been growing between them all day.

"What's that, my love?"

She tilted her head back a little, so that he could see the love in her eyes. "I'd say that our official honeymoon definitely begins tonight."

She laughed as Thomas wasted no time opening the door and scooping her up in his arms to carry her over the threshold.

THIRTY-THREE

Isabella yawned and turned over under the cozy down comforter. The morning view from the bedroom balcony that had gone unnoticed the night before was now displayed in front of her, and the magnificence of it nearly took her breath away.

"Good morning, my beautiful wife."

Not yet ready to get out of the very comfortable bed, she smiled and turned at the sound of Thomas's voice. He placed a cup of delicious-smelling coffee on the bedside table beside her before he leaned down to kiss her on the nose.

"Good morning, my handsome husband." She smiled and reached up to pull him down next to her on the bed. "And thank you for the coffee." She kissed him on the lips, which seemed persuasion enough for him to settle in beside her, pulling her close against him.

"How'd you sleep?" His fingers stroked her cheek and then pushed her hair gently back behind her ear.

Her body shivered at his touch. She grinned. "Maybe the best night's sleep I've ever had—and you?"

"It was fantastic. I thought I was dreaming for a moment this morning when I woke up to you lying beside me."

Isabella snuggled next to him under the covers. "It is a dream, I think. But I don't want to wake up."

"Iz, was everything alright—last night, I mean?"

Isabella felt her face go slightly warm, but it was only by habit. She didn't feel embarrassed talking to Thomas. She needed for him to know that he'd made her first experience beautiful and memorable—that it had been more special than she ever could have hoped for.

She told him as much, and then she did feel a bit shy all of a sudden. "What about you? Was it okay for you? I know that—"

Thomas kissed her, the look in his eyes undeniable—the look in his eyes telling her exactly how he felt about last night.

They lay in bed together for another hour after making love, talking about the villa and their plans for the vineyard. Remarkably, Rebecca had found someone who'd done a beautiful job furnishing the house. Thomas had hired her under the condition that everything would have to have a final okay from Isabella—and Isabella couldn't find one single thing she'd change as they walked through the house together in the light of day.

Thomas had slipped and told Isabella that they'd be on the late afternoon flight to Paris, to which she'd laughed and teased him that he was losing his touch. He'd laughed and said that apparently he had reached his quota for keeping secrets for a while.

Brunch wasn't until eleven, and it was still early as they sat at the breakfast table drinking coffee and talking.

"Shall we go for a walk? I'd love to show you the property," Thomas said.

"Yes, I'm dying to see it. Oh, and there's something I'd like to do—something I'd like us to do together." She grinned, as Thomas was on his feet before she'd even finished speaking.

"I know exactly where it is. I'll be right back." He kissed her on the lips before he left the room.

Somehow Thomas had already managed to have all their things shipped. Everything had already been put away.

Remarkably, the villa already felt like home to Isabella.

THIRTY-FOUR

Isabella stood with Thomas on what seemed to be the highest point of the property. There was a little slope to the yard, close enough that Isabella could imagine looking out from the kitchen window at children playing in the grass. She smiled at the thought and felt Thomas's hand tighten around hers.

"What do you think, Iz?"

"Oh, Thomas, I think it's beautiful—really beautiful."

"Good. I had a very strong suspicion that you'd like it here as much as I do." He grinned.

Isabella stretched her arms up high, feeling the sun on her face and the light breeze in her hair. "What do you think about this spot? It feels like we can see everything from here."

Thomas nodded and placed the single remaining small bag of Arianna's ashes in Isabella's palm. "Are you sure, Iz? That you don't want to keep some?"

Isabella thought about the question. She'd thought about keeping some of Arianna's ashes before but something about releasing her to the ground and wind here felt right. It felt like she'd been on a long journey with her mother, one that had led her to knowing Arianna, but maybe more importantly to her birth mother, it had been a journey to learning about herself.

Isabella shook her head. "No. This feels right to me."

She opened the small bag and scattered some of the ashes upon the ground where they stood. Then she took Thomas's hand in hers as she released the remaining ashes into the wind.

"Welcome home, Arianna."

EPILOGUE

~ Four Years Later ~

Isabella sat on the bench as she watched Thomas across the yard, his arms tanned and muscular, his smile wide as he waved at her. Isabella smiled and waved back, an intense feeling of complete contentment coming over her.

She ran her fingers over the engraved words along the bench. *In loving memory of Arianna Sinclair—The best journey leads you home.*

"We did it, Arianna." She whispered the words and took in the villa and vineyard all around her. They'd built a home here together—she and Thomas—filled with laughter and love, friendships and family—it was a dream come true for her, a life she'd only ever imagined having as a young girl.

"Mommyyyyyy!"

It was an instant—and welcomed—interruption from her pleasant thoughts.

Isabella laughed as her three-year-old daughter—dark pigtails flying behind her—came running toward her across the yard.

"Yes, honey? Be careful now. Don't run so fast. Remember what happened yesterday?"

She saw Thomas grin as the little girl stopped in her tracks to point to and examine the bright pink band-aid on her knee.

"I fell down but Daddy made it better." She erupted into giggles as Thomas ran up behind her, scooping her into his arms for several kisses before placing her on his shoulders.

Isabella laughed watching the pair as Thomas made his way toward her.

"Arianna, honey, hold on tight to daddy."

Thomas set the little girl on the bench in between them as he leaned over to give Isabella a quick kiss on the lips.

"Mommy?"

"Yes, honey?"

"How much longer until the girls get here? Our tea is getting cold."

"So, you're inviting the twins to one of your famous tea parties, are you?" Thomas asked.

"Yes, but Daisy doesn't like the tea—only me and Chloe drink the tea."

"What does Daisy like to drink, then?" Thomas asked, kissing the tip of his daughter's nose.

"Coffee—black." She turned toward Isabella. "But don't worry, Mommy. It's only pretend. Aunt Jemma really doesn't let Daisy drink coffee."

Isabella and Thomas both laughed at the same time and Isabella leaned down to kiss her daughter.

"Jemma and the twins should be here any minute. But honey, don't forget that everyone is coming—Blu, Kylie, Grandma Lia and Gabby—"

"—And Grandma Gigi and Grandpa Douglas?"

Isabella nodded.

"And Grandma and Grandpa that come on the airplane?"

"Yes, honey. Everyone's coming to celebrate your birthday today. Are you excited to be turning three?"

"Yes!"

Three already. Where had the years gone? As her daughter chattered about the party, Isabella reached behind her to massage her husband's neck just in the spot he liked her to. They caught one another's eye and smiled.

"Ari, honey?"

"Yes, Daddy."

"I think you should go set your table for a few more places, don't you? Maybe Kylie and Gabby are going to want to join your tea party, and you wouldn't want to be rude, would you?"

Arianna jumped off the bench. "Oh, Daddy! That's a great idea!" She started running toward her little table.

Isabella laughed as she scooted over toward Thomas. "Honey, stay where Daddy and I can see you in the yard."

Thomas reached out to take Isabella's hand and bring it to his lips. "How are you doing, love?"

"I'm fine. A little tired, maybe, but nothing a big family birthday party won't cure." She laughed and then shifted her weight suddenly. "Oh, Thomas!" She grinned and took his hand, placing it on her stomach. "Can you feel him?"

They were quiet for a few moments, Isabella holding still until their son kicked inside her once again. "There!"

Thomas grinned. "This one's gonna be a soccer player, I think."

They both laughed and Thomas's hand went to Isabella's cheek, turning her face gently toward his lips and his kiss that had only grown sweeter over the years.

"Iz, do you know how crazy about you I am?"

Isabella smiled. "If it's even half as much as I love you, darling, I'd say we're doing alright."

"I'd say we're doing alright then, my love." He kissed her again. "Much better than alright."

Thomas squeezed her hand and Isabella sighed.

Thomas laughed. "Was that a sigh of contentment or are you thinking about the nap you'd like to be taking?"

Isabella smiled as she watched their daughter play across the yard. "Total contentment."

THE STORY CONTINUES

Christmas in Tuscany
Legacy Series, Book 11

Available on Amazon

PaulaKayBooks.com

CHRISTMAS IN TUSCANY — PREVIEW

Chapter 1

Isabella smiled as she watched her daughter from across the room, her thick dark curls wild and framing the most beautiful face that Isabella had ever known.

Arianna.

The day that Isabella had married Thomas had been the happiest day of her life—until the day she'd given birth to their daughter. Three-year-old Arianna seemed to have them both wrapped around her little finger but she had such a sweet way about her—a disposition that made her a delight to be around.

"Arianna, honey? Are you sharing with the girls?"

Jemma's twins, Chloe and Daisy, seemed to be waiting patiently at the small table, while Arianna stood beside them with her tray of cookies.

"Mommy!" Arianna turned toward Isabella, her forehead creased. "I'm only trying to find the very best cookies for them. They aren't all the same, you know—and Daisy doesn't like the ones with nuts."

Isabella laughed and looked at Jemma, who was grinning

beside her on the sofa where Isabella sat opening a big box of Christmas ornaments. "Okay, honey. When you three finish your tea party, we're going to start decorating the tree, so don't go running off."

"We won't, Mommy."

Isabella placed her hand on her stomach as she felt the sharp kick from inside her. "Listen here, you little soccer player, don't get any wild ideas."

Jemma reached out to touch her arm. "Are you feeling okay? I can handle the three little *amigas* if you want to go lie down for a little bit."

"Thanks, Jem. I'm fine. I'm just not at all sure if this little guy of ours is going to wait until after Christmas to make his appearance. On the one hand, the closer to the due date the better; on the other, I feel as big as a house and my ankles might never be normal again, so you know—maybe get this child out of me already."

Both women laughed and Thomas entered the room, crossing it in quick even strides to sit down beside Isabella and pull her in for a hug, barely fitting his arm around her very large stomach.

"Oh, man. Be careful there, mister. I don't want to squish you." Isabella laughed and allowed herself to close her eyes and relax against the broad chest that had become home to her.

She felt Arianna's presence next to her, before she opened her eyes to see her daughter standing beside them, her little hands on her hips, studying them carefully.

"Mommy, please don't squish Daddy."

Thomas laughed. "Don't worry, honey. Daddy is too strong to be taken down so easily."

Arianna did not look convinced. "Daddy, look how big Mommy's tummy is."

Isabella laughed and sat up so that Thomas could pull Arianna up into his lap, his kisses smothering her face as she giggled, filling the room with the sound that brought them endless joy.

"Daddy, stop. Please." Arianna quieted herself enough to get the words out and then gently placed her head on Isabella's lap, turning her face toward Isabella's stomach. "Hello, little brother."

Isabella ran her fingers over her daughter's hair, careful not to get caught up in the tangles. She felt that overwhelming surge of love—the kind that seemed to literally make her heart beat faster. She'd never known love like the love she had for her daughter. Was it even possible that she could love their son—that they could love their son—even half as much? Everyone assured her that it was true about the depth of love for a child knowing no bounds—that their love would only expand as their family expanded.

She leaned down to kiss Arianna on the head. "Can you feel those kicks? I think your baby brother knows your voice, sweet girl."

Arianna sat up and put her hand gently on Isabella's stomach and then giggled. "I do, Mommy! I do feel him kicking. I wish he would come out soon."

Isabella looked at Thomas and then put her hand in his that reached for her. "I do too, honey. Any day now he's going to make his appearance."

Arianna kissed first Isabella on the lips and then reached for Thomas with a big hug and a quick kiss. "I have to go play with the twins now. They're waiting very patiently for me."

Thomas laughed and set her down on the floor. "Go ahead then. Have fun and play nice."

Arianna turned as if on cue, hands on her hips, which seemed to be a signature stance of hers lately. "Daddy! Why do you say that? You know I always play nice."

Thomas laughed, as did Isabella.

"Honey, you do play nice. Daddy is only kidding."

Thomas nodded his head and squeezed Isabella's hand as Arianna ran over to where the girls were playing. He pulled Isabella in for a kiss, wrapping his arms tightly around her.

"Ugh—I might not ever be able to get off you, you know," said Isabella.

Thomas kissed her on the nose as he looked into her eyes. "That is not so bad, my love. And have I told you how absolutely gorgeous you look today?"

Isabella smiled, thinking how just a moment earlier, she'd felt not the least bit gorgeous. Somehow Thomas made her feel like the most radiant woman in the room—always—no matter the crowd or circumstances. She always felt special when he looked at her, and after four years of marriage, that feeling of total love and adoration had only grown stronger between them.

"You're too sweet to me." She kissed him back. "Somehow I have to muster the energy to get the decorating done today. I promised the girls, and they can't wait to see the lights on the tree."

"Are you feeling okay, honey?" Thomas looked at his watch. "Maybe I can move my meeting and help you out here."

"No. No, it's okay. I'll be fine and Jemma is here. Maybe I will steal away for a small nap before Lia and Gigi come with lunch. Ooh, that sounds delightful, actually."

Thomas leaned down to kiss her on the neck—in just the place that he knew drove her crazy. "Maybe I have time to join you for that nap." He winked.

Isabella laughed. "I don't think so, honey. I mean, I really need to try to catch a little sleep." She tilted her head back a little to look at him. "But I'll certainly take a rain check on whatever it is you have in mind."

Her added weight and lack of energy did not keep her from wanting her husband. Thomas had only grown more romantic over the years, something that Isabella never tired of.

He grinned back at her and gently helped her to sit up before rising and reaching for her hands to help her up off the sofa.

"That's a deal. I shouldn't be gone long. Dinner is at Lia's tonight?"

"Yes, Mom and Dad get in around two, I think and—Jemma? What time is the rest of your gang coming?"

"Chase is coming with Kylie this afternoon. Mom has that show in Paris. I think she gets in tomorrow."

"And Rafael?" Thomas asked. "Have you heard from him how things are going?"

Just days earlier there had been an earthquake in Guatemala—one that had affected the orphanage. With Jemma's blessing and the promise to be back before Christmas day, Rafael had gotten a flight out straight after they'd heard the news.

"I spoke with him shortly after he arrived. Things aren't great but they've gotten a lot of help with the rebuilding—at least until they can get something more permanent in place. And no one at the orphanage was hurt, thank God."

Isabella sat down on the sofa next to her best friend, putting her arm around her. Jemma and the twins had come to stay with them the day that Rafael had left, and she knew that her friend had concerns that Rafael might not make it back in time for Christmas. Isabella knew that look on her friend's face. Jemma was worried.

"Are you okay?" Isabella said.

"Yeah. Well, I've texted Rafael a few times this morning and I haven't heard back from him.

Thomas walked over and placed a hand on Jemma's shoulder. "Don't worry, Jem. He'll get back in time."

Jemma smiled. "I know. I'm okay. Really. And the girls love being here."

"And I love having you here—you know that!" Isabella laughed.

"And on that note, my friend... Why don't you go have that nap I heard you mentioning? The girls seem pretty content right now and we can decorate the tree after."

Thomas held his hand out to Isabella and she grabbed it, letting him pull her to her feet.

"Well, I will not say no to that idea. Arianna? Mommy's going to go lie down for a few minutes. You mind Aunt Jemma, okay?"

"Okay, Mommy."

Thomas kissed her on the lips. "Have a nice rest, my darling. I'll see you all later this afternoon. Thanks, Jemma."

Isabella turned back toward Jemma before she made her way upstairs to the bedroom. "Thanks, Jem. I won't be long."

"No worries, Bella. Get a good rest while you can."

Chapter 2

After checking in on the girls, who seemed to be content playing house in one corner of the large family room, Jemma grabbed her phone and flopped down on the sofa. Still no word from Rafael. She bit her bottom lip as she punched in another text asking him if everything was alright. It wasn't like Rafael not to respond right away, and she was trying not to feel nervous about it.

She didn't have another second to think about it before she had an incoming call from her mother.

"Hi, Mom."

"Hi, honey. How's it going there?"

Blu's voice sounded strained to Jemma even in the few words that were spoken, and it was very noisy in the background.

"Everything's good. I'm just hanging out with the girls while Bella has a little nap. How's the show going?"

Blu said something that Jemma couldn't make out.

"Mom, I'm having a hard time hearing you. Can you say that again?"

"Let me step outside for a minute."

Jemma waited the few seconds that it took for the line to grow much quieter.

"Sorry, honey. It's a bit crazy here right now, but things are winding down. I was asking you—honey, have you had the news on? Have you heard from Rafael?"

"No, I haven't and I'd be lying if I said I wasn't getting concerned. I know he's busy there right now but it's just not like him..." Jemma suddenly realized how silent her mom was on the other end of the line. "Mom? What's on the news? Has something else happened?" She felt her heartbeat quicken as she waited for Blu to respond.

"Jem, I'm sure he's fine—"

"Mom, you're scaring me."

Jemma saw Chloe's eyes on her from across the room and attempted to quiet her voice. The last thing she wanted was for the twins to see her upset about Rafael. They'd already expressed their fears that their father was going to be away from them at Christmas. She turned her head slightly so that the girls could no longer read the emotions on her face. "Mom, what is it?"

"Honey, there's been another earthquake—a pretty big one, I'm afraid. But I think it's also affected communications—they said that on the news—that a lot of the phone and Internet might be down now. I'm sure you'll be hearing from him soon that everything is alright."

Jemma felt her breath catch in her throat. She couldn't bear it if anything happened to Rafael. She could hardly remember her life without him and the girls—he just had to be okay. But why wasn't he answering her texts?

"Honey? Are you okay? Is someone there with you now? Jemma, try not to think the worst. I'm sure you'll hear from him soon."

Jemma took a deep breath in and willed herself to answer. "Yes, I'm okay. I mean, I'm not but I guess I just need to keep trying to get a hold of him. Bella's resting upstairs but Lia and Gigi are due any time for lunch."

"I'm sorry, but they're calling me to come back inside. Please text me as soon as you hear anything, and I'm going to call you back as soon as I'm done here, okay?"

"Okay, don't worry. I'm alright." It was a lie but Jemma didn't want Blu worrying about her when she was right in the middle of a big event.

"I love you, honey. Talk to Bella and the others—tell them

what's happened, and I'm sure Douglas can help you find out what's going on."

"Okay, yes, that's a good idea. Bye, Mom."

Jemma felt her daughter's hand on her arm as she hung up the phone.

"What's wrong, Mommy?" It was Chloe, always so sensitive to feelings that were swirling around her. Sometimes Jemma actually wondered if the young girl had some kind of psychic ability—she was often that much in tune to the emotions of others.

"Nothing's wrong, honey. Are you girls almost ready for some lunch?"

"Mommy, don't fib."

Jemma laughed despite her still worried thoughts. "Honey, I'm not fibbing. Why do you say that, silly?"

"I can tell. I can always tell when you're not telling me the complete story."

Jemma leaned in to kiss her daughter on the forehead. Chloe was repeating the very same words that her father had used with her days earlier when he'd caught her lying about something that had happened between her and Daisy.

"Honey, there's no story to tell. Go tell Daisy and Ari that it's time to clean up now. And I'll go get those delicious sandwiches you helped me make earlier."

"And the fruit salad?"

Jemma smiled. "Yes, I won't forget the fruit salad."

Chloe, seemingly satisfied enough to forget the grilling of her mother for information—for now, anyway—ran off to join the other girls.

Jemma watched her run off and then saw Chloe put her arm around her sister, her worried thoughts momentarily interrupted by the physical love she had for her daughters. Twins. She still marveled at it. It seemed impossible that they'd gone through her whole pregnancy without the knowledge that there were two little girls vying for attention in her womb.

She had panicked only for a second when the doctor had told them the news during the delivery—only for that very brief second, before she saw the tears in Rafael's eyes. He'd leaned down to kiss her, squeezing her hand and telling her that everything was going to be just fine—that two babies were just perfect for their family.

First there was Chloe—a name they'd chosen quite easily—followed by her sister. Jemma had gazed down at her with wonder as Rafael held their firstborn and just like that, the name Daisy had come to her and seemed to suit their little surprise daughter perfectly.

Now that they were four, it seemed that every day Jemma noticed the distinct differences between her daughters. Chloe, the eldest by mere seconds, was always the big sister—slightly bossy, and with a watchful eye that seemed to always be on her sister. She was definitely the more vocal of the two.

Daisy was quieter than her sister, but had an equally loud voice when it came to expressing her displeasure over something. She was intensely loyal, never one to tattle, a trait that Jemma found especially endearing. Daisy could play outside for hours; Jemma would often find her under the big tree outside with a favorite book in her hand. Daisy also loved to paint, and while trying not to be biased, Jemma felt that there was definitely some natural talent there.

Yes, their daughters had brought great pleasure to their lives.

Jemma felt the jolt of panic once again as she looked down at her phone screen. *Raf, please text me.* 12:30. Lia and Gigi would be there in a half hour and Isabella was likely to be up before then. She'd just busy herself with the girls and their lunch and try to put any worrisome thoughts out of her mind.

Rafael would be fine. He'd be home for Christmas just like he'd promised Jemma and the girls. Everything would be fine. Jemma recited the words inside her head as if it was a mantra of positive thoughts she could will into fruition.

A NOTE FROM THE AUTHOR

Thank you so much for reading *Bella's Home*.

If you've fallen in love with these characters and the world of the Legacy Series, I'd love to invite you deeper into the story.

I've written a quiet, emotional prequel titled *Out of Time* that sheds light on the relationships, choices, and moments that shaped everything that follows.

As a thank-you for joining my reader list, you can receive *Out of Time* as a free digital gift, along with future updates and special releases from the Legacy Series and my other women's fiction.

To receive your free prequel, please visit:
PaulaKayBooks.com

I'm so glad you're here.
—Paula

ABOUT THE AUTHOR

Paula Kay writes women's fiction about family, friendship, and the quiet moments that shape who we become.

Her Legacy Series explores love, loss, and the ties that bind us across generations, with settings inspired by Italy, San Francisco, and the places that feel like home long after we've left them behind.

When she's not writing, Paula enjoys meaningful conversations, books that make her cry, and a little too much reality television.

PaulaKayBooks.com

ALSO BY PAULA KAY

Legacy Series:

Book 1: *Buying Time*

Book 2: *In Her Own Time*

Book 3: *Matter of Time*

Book 4: *Taking Time*

Book 5: *Just in Time*

Book 6: *All in Good Time*

Book 7: *Bella's Hope*

Book 8: *Bella's Holiday*

Book 9: *Bella's Heart*

Book 10: *Bella's Home*

Book 11: *Christmas in Tuscany: A Legacy Series Reunion*

Book 12: *Birthday Surprise: A Legacy Series Reunion*

Book 13: *A Summer Together: A Legacy Series Reunion*

Book 14: *In This Moment: A Legacy Series Reunion*

Book 15: *Where It Began: A Legacy Series Reunion*

The Nomadic Sisterhood:

Know by Heart

Stay the Course

Clear the Air

Lost for Words

Out of Touch

Turn the Tide

Rock the Boat

Back on Track